SUNG
UNDER THE
SILVER UMBRELLA

THE UMBRELLA BOOKS

TOLD UNDER THE
GREEN UMBRELLA

TOLD UNDER THE
BLUE UMBRELLA

SUNG UNDER THE
SILVER UMBRELLA

TOLD UNDER THE
MAGIC UMBRELLA

TOLD UNDER THE
STARS AND STRIPES

TOLD UNDER THE
CHRISTMAS TREE

TOLD UNDER
SPACIOUS SKIES

SING-SONG, RHYTHM AND RHYME
THE BEST IN CHILDREN'S POETRY

SUNG
UNDER THE
SILVER UMBRELLA

Selected by the Literature Committee of the
Association for Childhood Education International

Illustrated by Dorothy Lathrop

THE MACMILLAN COMPANY · NEW YORK · 1962
A Division of The Crowell-Collier Publishing Company

TO

ALL CHILDREN

WHO LOVE

TO

DANCE AND SING AND PLAY

FOREWORD

THE making of poems for childhood is a very delicate un-
dertaking. It is like domesticating a creature of the wild.
The creature domesticated is a mood or impression; it is the
poet's wonder, his discovery that what he has been looking
at is unique. I dwell on the word domesticated, for the poem
made for childhood has to be lived with more familiarly
than the poem made for grown-up people; the mood or the
impression has to be made completely domestic. The old
nursery rhymes did this perfectly:

> *Goosey-goosey gander,*
> *Where do you wander?*
> *Upstairs and downstairs*
> *And to my lady's chamber.*

Here the inquiring and exploring aimlessness which is goosi-
ness in its essence is given in swift, bold strokes. And it is
idle for us to exclaim that one does not enter into conversation with a goose one meets on a stairway, and that if one
does he does not get such a well-worded answer. The wonder has been felt, the impression rendered; that wild, winged
thing, the goose of all time, has been domesticated completely.

In an enormous lot of verse intended for childhood there
is a fault—it domesticates the domestic. Plates and clocks and
pinafores are just plates and clocks and pinafores; the impression of them as unique things has not been rendered in
arresting measures. The makers of them have not been

[ix]

aroused to a discovery as has one of the poets represented here by hearing how hens talk before they go to sleep:

One of them moved and turned around,
Her feathers made a ruffled sound,

A ruffled sound, like a bushful of birds,
And she said her little asking words.

One of the merits of this collection is that it does not domesticate the domestic.

Poetry exists that we may have an accompaniment to our thoughts—something rhythmical, liberated, of another dimension going along with our accustomed toil, pastime and distraction. At all periods of our lives we have need of this accompaniment; we have particular need of it, judging by the way we demand it then, in the period of infancy and childhood. Hence "Ring-a-ring-a-rosy" and "Oranges, oranges, four for a penny," and all the play-rhymes that children who have not been brought up in solitude know; hence the universality and immortality of Mother Goose's rhymes.

Of course these are to be distinguished from poetry— Mother Goose's are rhymes merely. But they do for our unreflective days what high poetry should do for our reflective days—they make an accompaniment for the thoughts of childhood, they put alongside the active and practical lives of children the rhythmical, liberated accompaniment. There is a stage in our lives when knowledge of the world and types of human character have to come to us as a legend, as a piece of mythology, and it is natural and fitting that they should come to us in rhyme:

The King was in his counting-house,
Counting out his money,
The Queen was in her parlor
Eating bread and honey.

[x]

Kings and Queens should exist for us in this handsomeness and opulence before they exist for us as heads of states, and the rhyming way is surely the proper way of introduction to such personalities. Then, too, there is an oral stage in our lives when our minds are receptive to words, when words naturally take the form of rhymes, and when rhymes become a favorite possession. Rhymes that give some impression, that hold some mood, should be around us then—poems of the kind that can enter the mind of a child and remain one of its possessions.

In the old days the rhymes that made report of the world and went to form the gallery of human characters—Mother Hubbard, Simple Simon and the rest of the well-remembered procession—came from nurses who had no book knowledge and who brought everything they gave out of an oral tradition. Nowadays children have poems taught them by well read instructors. If I were amongst such pedagogues I should have children learn by heart a great deal of verse. The more verse they hold in their minds the more mental and imaginative capital they possess. And the more points of focus they have for actualizing other material—philosophical or scientific material as might be the case. Also, the possession of verse with its sound and its pattern would give them a notion of the enchantment and the music that is in language itself. But I would have the children learn verse orally, not from eyeing a book but from someone's recital or reading. This, however, brings up a problem; how, in delivering it to the children, is verse to be said? How is it to be repeated by them? Certainly not in the sing-song nor galloping way that children are likely to repeat verses that they learned out of books, nor yet in the elocutionary style with all that underlining by tone and gesture to add meaning to words, which being the words of experts need no such additions. I am thinking at the moment of three poems by different poets each of which gives the mood of a part of the day. The first is the morning mood; it is by Eleanor Farjeon:

> *The tapping of sticks*
> *And the patter of feet,*
> *The wind in the plane-trees*
> *That whisper and rustle,*
> *The pigeons all sleepy,*
> *The newsboys all hustle,*
> *The* clippety-clop
> *And the* clip-clop *again*
> *Of soldiers and horses,*
> *More horses than men.*

And then there is James Stephens that gives us the pause of the evening:

> *At eve the horse is freed of plough or wain,*
> *And turns from labour unto yearnéd rest!*

And afterwards comes the mystery and glamour of night in Walter de la Mare's:

> *Slowly, silently, now the moon*
> *Walks the night in her silver shoon.*

The music that conveys the rise of the morning, the pause of the evening, the presence of the night, is as different as any music that can be given in words. The essential music that is in each should be revealed by one who appreciates it. The child who takes one or the three of these poems into his or her mind should feel that music. And the problem is to get the children to feel it. A simple but intelligent reading could help them. But the sing-song, the galloping, the elocutionary should be discouraged. One of the things to do would be to let the children discover that what they are asked to like is of the same species with what they have —their own play-rhymes—and is not an alien thing.

I have said that one of the merits of this collection is that it does not domesticate the domestic; every piece in it has come out of a discovery. Another of its merits is in its abundance; it is a good idea to give children a full volume— something they can move about in and make a world of their own out of. The known, the less known, and the unknown poets are here in fair proportion. And the student of literature who goes through the volume will have interest in noting how finely contemporary poets continue the tradition of making poetry for children.

That tradition is amongst the most recent of literary traditions; it is less than a hundred years old, dating only from after the middle of the nineteenth century. Before that there were only traditional rhymes and songs and pious and cautionary verses. Then there came the poems of William Allingham and Christina Rossetti—genuine poems for an audience of children. But it is not from these, delightful as they are and classics that they are of their kind, that the type of poetry we have in mind when we speak of poetry for children has come. This particular kind has its origin in *Alice in Wonderland, A Child's Garden of Verses*, and Edwin Lear's *Nonsense Verses* which were not made especially for children. The present collection shows how contemporary poets have enriched the fine, if recent, tradition of poetry for childhood. Here is Walter de la Mare, who always himself, always the most distinctive of modern poets, gives us not a fairy tale but the essence of a fairy tale, in his lovely verses for the young; here is James Stephens who has turned from King and Queen to Eirinn to give a wonderful luminousness to a child's day; here is Eleanor Farjeon, who gives every scene she brings before us the color and movement and excitement of a fair; here is Vachel Lindsay whose verses have the very vocalization of the play-rhyme; here is Edna Millay, who gives us a child's lonely adventurousness. There are a score of others whose distinctive quality I feel without being able to define it. But I am moved to speak of two of them. There is Elizabeth Madox Roberts, who can give us the mysterious world that is at the edge of the farm:

> *And far away and far away—*
> *I wonder if the farmer man*
> *Knows all about the corn and how*
> *It comes together like a fan.*

And there is Elizabeth Coatsworth, whose sympathy with the little creatures of the wild is so moving that she makes us heartily ashamed of the niggardliness of our dealings with our little housemates, the mice:

> *"Moonlight is there*
> *And a bare place for dancing,*
> *But no little feast*
> *Is spread any more."*

The poems by every one of these poets is a welcome and a good-wish to those who would come "under the Silver Umbrella."

PADRAIC COLUM

CONTENTS

[xv]

Gold locks, and black locks,
Red locks and brown.

Then out a-shin-shan-shining
In the bright blue day.

About
And roundabout.

And so has a crocodile, and so
    Has a quail—
They've all got tails but me!

All to the haven
Where each would be,
Fly!

[xvii]

Laughing with friends,
I'm always sorry
When the ride ends.

Minnie and Mattie
And fat little May,
Out in the country,
Spending the day.

[xviii]

Awake! Oh, North Wind,
And come, thou South,
Blow you upon my garden.

[xix]

Suppose—
And suppose.

Wee folk, good folk
Trooping all together.

Where we walk to school each day
Indian children used to play.

Come, choose your road
And away!

And everything that's mine
Is yours, and yours, and yours.

Sing a song of seasons!
Something bright in all!

[xxi]

Come Christmas the morn!

Good night! good night!
Far flies the light.

"HIGGLEDY PIGGLEDY, O!"

Mix a pancake,
Stir a pancake,
    Pop it in the pan;
Fry the pancake,
Toss the pancake,—
    Catch it if you can.

                    —*Christina G. Rossetti*

What does the bee do?
    Bring home honey.
And what does Father do?
    Bring home money.
And what does Mother do?
    Lay out the money.
And what does baby do?
    Eat up the honcy.

                    —*Christina G. Rossetti*

MARY MIDDLING

Mary Middling had a pig,
Not very little and not very big,
Not very pink, not very green,
Not very dirty, not very clean,
Not very good, not very naughty,
Not very humble, not very haughty,
Not very thin, not very fat;
Now what would you give for a pig like that?

                    —*Rose Fyleman*

PICNIC

Ella, fell a
Maple tree.
Hilda, build a
Fire for me.

Teresa, squeeze a
Lemon, so.
Amanda, hand a
Plate to Flo.

Nora, pour a
Cup of tea.
Fancy, Nancy,
What a spree!
—*Hugh Lofting*

THE FUNNY OLD MAN AND HIS WIFE

Once upon a time, in a little wee house,
    Lived a funny old man and his wife;
And he said something funny to make her laugh,
    Every day of his life.

One day he said such a very funny thing,
    That she shook and scream'd with laughter;
But the poor old soul, she couldn't leave off
    For at least three whole days after.

So laughing with all her might and main,
    Three days and nights she sat;
And at the end she didn't know a bit
    What she'd been laughing at.
—*Author Unknown*

[4]

A NONSENSE ALPHABET

A

A was once an apple-pie,
>Pidy,
>Widy,
>Tidy,
>Pidy,

Nice insidy,
Apple-pie!

B

B was once a little bear,
>Beary,
>Wary,
>Hairy,
>Beary,

Taky cary,
Little bear!

C

C was once a little cake,
>Caky,
>Baky,
>Maky,
>Caky,

Taky caky,
Little cake!

D

D was once a little doll,
>Dolly,
>Molly,
>Polly,
>Nolly,

Nursy dolly,
Little doll!

E

E was once a little eel,
    Eely,
    Weely,
    Peely,
    Eely,
Twirly, tweely,
Little eel!

F

F was once a little fish,
    Fishy,
    Wishy,
    Squishy,
    Fishy,
In a dishy,
Little fish!

G

G was once a little goose,
    Goosy,
    Moosy,
    Boosy,
    Goosy,
Waddly-woosy,
Little goose!

H

H was once a little hen,
    Henny,
    Chenny,
    Tenny,
    Henny,
Eggsy-any,
Little hen!

I

I was once a bottle of ink,
    Inky,
    Dinky,
    Thinky,
    Inky,
  Blacky minky,
  Bottle of ink!

J

J was once a jar of jam,
    Jammy,
    Mammy,
    Clammy,
    Jammy,
  Sweety, swammy,
  Jar of jam!

K

K was once a little kite,
    Kity,
    Whity,
    Flighty,
    Kity,
  Out of sighty,
  Little kite!

L

L was once a little lark,
    Larky,
    Marky,
    Harky,
    Larky,
  In the parky,
  Little lark!

M

M was once a little mouse,
　　Mousy,
　　Bousy,
　　Sousy,
　　Mousy,
　In the housy,
　Little mouse!

N

N was once a little needle,
　　Needly,
　　Tweedly,
　　Threedly,
　　Needly,
　Wiskly, wheedly,
　Little needle!

O

O was once a little owl,
　　Owly,
　　Prowly,
　　Howly,
　　Owly,
　Browny fowly,
　Little owl!

P

P was once a little pump,
　　Pumpy,
　　Slumpy,
　　Flumpy,
　　Pumpy,
　Dumpy, thumpy,
　Little pump!

Q

Q was once a little quail,
 Quaily,
 Faily,
 Daily,
 Quaily,
 Stumpy-taily,
 Little quail!

R

R was once a little rose,
 Rosy,
 Posy,
 Nosy,
 Rosy,
 Blows-y, grows-y,
 Little rose!

S

S was once a little shrimp,
 Shrimpy,
 Nimpy,
 Flimpy,
 Shrimpy,
 Jumpy, jimpy,
 Little shrimp!

T

T was once a little thrush,
 Thrushy,
 Hushy,
 Bushy,
 Thrushy,
 Flitty, flushy,
 Little thrush!

U

U was once a little urn,
    Urny,
    Burny,
    Turny,
    Urny,
Bubbly, burny,
Little urn!

V

V was once a little vine,
    Viny,
    Winy,
    Twiny,
    Viny,
Twisty-twiny,
Little vine!

W

W was once a whale,
    Whaly,
    Scaly,
    Shaly,
    Whaly,
Tumbly-taily,
Mighty whale!

X

X was once a great king Xerxes,
    Xerxy,
    Perxy,
    Turxy,
    Xerxy,
Linxy, lurxy,
Great King Xerxes!

Y

Y was once a little yew,
    Yewdy,
    Fewdy,
    Crudy,
    Yewdy,
Growdy, grewdy,
Little yew!

Z

Z was once a piece of zinc,
    Tinky,
    Winky,
    Blinky,
    Tinky,
Tinkly, minky,
Piece of zinc!

—*Edward Lear*

Five little monkeys
Swinging from a tree;
Teasing Uncle Crocodile,
Merry as can be.
Swinging high, swinging low,
Swinging left and right:
"Dear Uncle Crocodile,
Come and take a bite!"

Five little monkeys
Swinging in the air;
Heads up, tails up,
Little do they care.
Swinging up, swinging down,
Swinging far and near:
"Poor Uncle Crocodile,
Aren't you hungry, dear?"

Four little monkeys
Sitting in the tree;
Heads down, tails down,
Dreary as can be,
Weeping loud, weeping low,
Crying to each other:
"Wicked Uncle Crocodile,
To gobble up our brother!"

—*Laura E. Richards*

THE MERRY MAN OF PARIS

There is a little man
All dressed in grey,
He lives in Paris,
And he's always gay.

He's round as an apple,
And plump as a pear,
He hasn't a penny,
And he hasn't a care.

And he says, "I laugh,
And I laugh, and my plan,"
Says he, "is to laugh
And to laugh all I can!"
Oh! what a merry little fat grey man!

If the rain through his roof
His chamber-floor wets,
In his bed snugly lying
The rain he forgets.

In dreary December
It hails and it snows;
If fuel be wanting
His fingers he blows;

And he says, "I laugh,
And I laugh, and my plan,"
Says he, "is to laugh,
And to laugh all I can!"
Oh! what a merry little fat grey man!

—*Stella Mead*
After Béranger

JUMBO JEE

There were some kings, in number three,
Who built the tower of Jumbo Jee.
They built it up to a monstrous height,
At eleven o'clock on a Thursday night.

They built it up for forty miles,
With mutual bows and pleasing smiles;
And then they sat on the edge to rest,
And partook of lunch with a cheerful zest.

And first they ate of the porkly pie,
And wondered why they had built so high;
And next they drank of the ginger wine,
Which gave their noses a regal shine.

They drank to the health of Jumbo Jee,
Until they could neither hear nor see.
They drank to the health of Jumbo Land,
Until they could neither walk nor stand.

They drank to the health of Jumbo Tower
Until they really could drink no more;
And then they sank in a blissful swoon,
And flung their crowns at the rising moon.
                                   —*Laura E. Richards*

THE TALE OF A TART

Roly! poly! pudding and pie!
Who picked the apples and made them cry?
 " 'Twas we, 'twas we!"
Said little maids three;
"We picked the apples and made them cry."

Able, table! platter and cup!
Who peeled the apples and cut them up?
 "I," said the cook;
 "I gave them a look,
And whipped out my knife and cut them up."

Who made the tart? and who baked the tart?
 "The cook was the maker,
 But I," said the baker,
"I baked the tart for my little sweetheart."
    —Frederick E. Weatherley

THE HIGH BARBAREE

As I was sailing down the coast
 Of High Barbaree,
I chanced to see a Muffin Bird
 A-sitting in a tree.

Oh, mournfully he sang,
 And sorrowful he sat,
Because he was a-frightened of
 The Crumpet Cat!

[15]

The Crumpet Cat is little known;
    He sits him under trees,
And watches for the Muffin Bird
    His palate for to please.

And then he opens wide his mouth,
    The cruel Crumpet Cat,
And the Muffin Bird falls into it,
    Just—like—*that!*

I left the ship, I gained the shore,
    And to the tree I hied,
Just as the Cat was opening
    His jaws wide, wide!

I waved my arms and shouted loud,
    "Shoo! *shoo!* SHOO!"
And off the Cat went flumpering,
    And off the birdie flew.

Moral

When you sail the Barbaree,
    Mind what you're about!
Always carry with you
    A good loud shout!

When you see a Crumpet Cat,
    Let your shout be heard;
For you may save the life of
    A pretty Muffin Bird!

"Sailing down along the coast
Of the High Barbaree."
                    Old Song—*Laura E. Richards*

THE OWL AND THE PUSSY CAT

The Owl and the Pussy cat went to sea
  In a beautiful pea-green boat:
They took some honey, and plenty of money
  Wrapped up in a five-pound note.
The Owl looked up to the stars above,
  And sang to a small guitar,
"O lovely Pussy, O Pussy, my love,
What a beautiful Pussy you are,
         You are,
         You are!
What a beautiful Pussy you are!"

Pussy said to the Owl, "You elegant fowl,
  How charmingly sweet you sing!
Oh! let us be married; too long we have tarried:
  But what shall we do for a ring?"
They sailed away, for a year and a day
  To the land where the bong-tree grows,
And there in a wood a Piggy-wig stood,
  With a ring at the end of his nose,
         His nose,
         His nose,
With a ring at the end of his nose.

"Dear Pig, are you willing to sell for one shilling
  Your ring?" Said the Piggy, "I will."
So they took it away, and were married next day
  By the Turkey who lives on the hill.

They dinèd on mince and slices of quince,
  Which they ate with a runcible spoon,
  And hand in hand, on the edge of the sand,
  They danced by the light of the moon,
      The moon,
      The moon,
  They danced by the light of the moon.

—*Edward Lear*

"IN THIS TWEENY LITTLE, COZY
LITTLE HOUSE OF MINE!"

A SUMMER MORNING

I saw dawn creep across the sky,
And all the gulls go flying by.
I saw the sea put on its dress
Of blue mid-summer loveliness,
And heard the trees begin to stir
Green arms of pine and juniper.
I heard the wind call out and say:
"Get up, my dear, it is to-day!"

—Rachel Field

Softly, drowsily,
Out of sleep;
Into the world again
Ann's eyes peep;
Over the pictures
Across the walls
One little quivering
Sunbeam falls.
A thrush in the garden
Seems to say,
Wake, Little Ann,
'Tis day, 'tis day;
Faint sweet breezes
The casement stir
Breathing of pinks
And lavender,
At last from her pillow,
With cheeks bright red,
Up comes her round little
Tousled head;
And out she tumbles
From her warm bed.

—Walter de la Mare

THE SOUNDS IN THE MORNING

The sounds in the morning
Go all down the street:
The tapping of sticks
And the patter of feet,
The wind in the plane-trees
That whisper and rustle,
The pigeons all sleepy,
The newsboys all hustle,
The *clippety-clop*
And the *clip-clop* again
Of soldiers and horses,
More horses than men,
The clatter of milk-cans,
The chatter of maids,
The slop of their buckets,
The sort without spades,
And sometimes the mooing
Of slow-moving cows
Brings the smell of the lowlands
To me as I drowse,
And sometimes the bleating
And scuffle of sheep
Draws down the high hill-tops
To me half-asleep,
Dogs barking, bells chiming,
The twitter of sparrows—
Till the sun through the slats
Of my blind shoots his arrows,
And the world of my ears
Seems to dwindle in size
As I jump out of bed
To the world of my eyes.

—*Eleanor Farjeon*

[22]

NEW SHOES

I have new shoes in the Fall-time
And new ones in the Spring.
Whenever I wear my new shoes
I always have to sing!

—*Alice Wilkins*

CHOOSING SHOES

New shoes, new shoes,
    Red and pink and blue shoes.
Tell me, what would *you* choose,
    If they'd let us buy?

Buckle shoes, bow shoes,
    Pretty pointy-toe shoes,
Strappy, cappy low shoes;
    Let's have some to try.

Bright shoes, white shoes,
    Dandy-dance-by-night shoes,
Perhaps-a-little-tight shoes,
    Like some? So would I.

But

Flat shoes, fat shoes,
    Stump-along-like-that shoes,
Wipe-them-on-the-mat shoes,
    That's the sort they'll buy.

—*ffrida Wolfe*

BREAKFAST TIME

The sun is always in the sky
Whenever I get out of bed,
And I often wonder why
It's never late.—My sister said

She didn't know who did the trick,
And that she didn't care a bit,
And I should eat my porridge quick.
... I think its mother wakens it.

—*James Stephens*

MISS T.

It's a very odd thing—
    As odd as can be—
That whatever Miss T. eats
    Turns into Miss T.;
Porridge and apples,
    Mince, muffins, and mutton,
Jam, junket, jumbles—
    Not a rap, not a button
It matters; the moment
    They're out of her plate,
Though shared by Miss Butcher
    And sour Mr. Bate,
Tiny and cheerful,
    And neat as can be,
Whatever Miss T. eats
    Turns into Miss T.

—*Walter de la Mare*

[24]

"SH"

"Sh!" says mother,
"Sh!" says father.
"Running in the hall
Is a very great bother.

"Mrs. Grumpy Grundy,
Who lives down below,
Will come right up
First thing you know."

"Sh!" says father,
"Sh!" says mother.
"Can't you play a quiet game
Of some kind or other?"

—*James S. Tippett*

HIDING

I'm hiding, I'm hiding,
And no one knows where;
For all they can see is my
Toes and my hair.

And I just heard my father
Say to my mother—
"But, darling, he must be
Somewhere or other;

Have you looked in the inkwell?"
And Mother said, "Where?"
"In the INKWELL?" said Father. But
I was not there.

Then "Wait!" cried my mother—
"I think that I see
Him under the carpet." But
It was not me.

"Inside the mirror's
A pretty good place,"
Said Father and looked, but saw
Only his face.

"We've hunted," sighed Mother,
"As hard as we could
And I AM so afraid that we've
Lost him for good."

Then I laughed out aloud
And I wiggled my toes
And Father said—"Look, dear,
I wonder if those

Toes could be Benny's?
There are ten of them, see?"
And they WERE so surprised to find
Out it was me!

—Dorothy Aldis

FUN IN A GARRET

We're having a lovely time to-day!
We're all of us up in the garret at play!
We have three houses under the eaves—
Not real, you know, but make-believes.
Two we live in, and one is a store,
Where a little old screen makes a truly door.

Warren keeps store, and Joe is his clerk.
And Betty and I stay home and work.
Joe comes around and knocks or rings,
And we order potatoes and steaks and things,
And sometimes we go to the store and buy,
Or send the children for ribbons or pie.

It's lots of fun—just try it some day
When it rains too hard to go out to play.
                                        —*Emma C. Dowd*

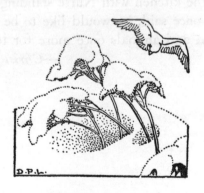

ANIMAL CRACKERS

Animal crackers, and cocoa to drink,
That is the finest of suppers, I think;
When I'm grown up and can have what I please
I think I shall always insist upon these.

What do *you* choose when you're offered a treat?
When Mother says, "What would you like best to eat?"
Is it waffles and syrup, or cinnamon toast?
It's cocoa and animals that *I* love the most!

The kitchen's the cosiest place that I know:
The kettle is singing, the stove is aglow,
And there in the twilight, how jolly to see
The cocoa and animals waiting for me.

Daddy and Mother dine later in state,
With Mary to cook for them, Susan to wait;
But they don't have nearly as much fun as I
Who eat in the kitchen with Nurse standing by;
And Daddy once said, he would like to be me
Having cocoa and animals once more for tea!

—*Christopher Morley*

THE SHINY LITTLE HOUSE

I wish, how I wish, that I had a little house,
With a mat for the cat and a hole for a mouse,
And a clock going "tock" in a corner of the room
And a kettle, and a cupboard, and a big birch broom.

To school in the morning the children off would run,
And I'd give them a kiss and a penny and a bun.
But directly they had gone from this little house of mine,
I'd clasp my hands and snatch a cloth, and shine, shine, shine.

I'd shine all the knives, all the windows and the floors,
All the grates, all the plates, all the handles on the doors,
Every fork, every spoon, every lid, and every tin,
Till everything was shining like a new bright pin.

At night, by the fire, when the children were in bed,
I'd sit and I'd knit, with a cap upon my head,
And the kettles, and the saucepans they would shine, shine,
    shine,
In this tweeny little, cosy little house of mine!

—*Nancy M. Hayes*

AN EVENING FALLS

(1)

At eve the horse is freed of plough or wain,
And turns from labour into yearnéd rest:

The scattered sheep are gathering home again!
The crow is winging to a lovéd nest;

And to the den, in hedge or hill, once more
Go all who may:

(2)

Each mother listens now! Each is aware
That little feet have paused in field or street;

And she will hear
A knocking at the door

And open it,
And see her children there!

—*James Stephens*

"GOLD LOCKS, AND BLACK LOCKS, RED LOCKS AND BROWN."

LITTLE

I am the sister of him
And he is my brother.
He is too little for us
To talk to each other.

So every morning I show him
My doll and my book;
But every morning he still is
Too little to look.

—Dorothy Aldis

MY ZIPPER SUIT

My zipper suit is bunny-brown—
The top zips up, the legs zip down.
I wear it every day.
My daddy brought it out from town.
Zip it up, and zip it down,
And hurry out to play!

—Marie Louise Allen

THE MITTEN SONG
(to be chanted)

"Thumbs in the thumb-place,
Fingers all together!"
This is the song
We sing in mitten-weather.
When it is cold,
It doesn't matter whether
Mittens are wool,
Or made of finest leather.
This is the song
We sing in mitten-weather:
"Thumbs in the thumb-place,
Fingers all together!"

—Marie Louise Allen

[33]

TO LADDIE

Whistle, Laddie, whistle,
Whistle when the dawn,
Dances in the shadows,
Gay-hearted as a fawn.

Whistle, Laddie, whistle,
Whistle merrily;
Whistle for the red-wing
And the chickadee.

Whistle, Laddie, whistle,
While the fireflies spark,
Truer, clearer, louder,
Whistle through the dark.
—*Anne Robinson*

BUNCHES OF GRAPES

"Bunches of grapes," says Timothy;
  "Pomegranates pink," says Elaine;
"A junket of cream and a cranberry tart
  For me," says Jane.

"Love-in-a-mist," says Timothy;
  "Primroses pale," says Elaine;
"A nosegay of pinks and mignonette
  For me," says Jane.

"Chariots of gold," says Timothy;
  "Silvery wings," says Elaine;
"A bumpity ride in a wagon of hay
  For me," says Jane.
—*Walter de la Mare*

GIRLS' NAMES

What lovely names for girls there are!
There's Stella like the Evening Star,
And Sylvia like a rustling tree,
And Lola like a melody,
And Flora like a flowery morn,
And Sheila like a field of corn,
And Melusina like the moan
Of water. And there's Joan, like Joan.

—*Eleanor Farjeon*

BOYS' NAMES

What splendid names for boys there are!
There's Carol like a rolling car,
And Martin like a flying bird,
And Adam like the Lord's First Word,
And Raymond like the Harvest Moon,
And Peter like a piper's tune,
And Alan like the flowing on
Of water. And there's John, like John.

—*Eleanor Farjeon*

THE BARBER'S

Gold locks, and black locks,
    Red locks and brown,
Topknot to love-curl,
    The hair wisps down;
Straight above the clear eyes,
    Rounded round the ears,
Snip-snap and snick-a-snick,
    Clash the Barber's shears;
Us, in the looking-glass,
    Footsteps in the street,
Over, under, to and fro,
    The lean blades meet;
Bay Rum or Bear's Grease,
    A silver groat to pay—
Then out a-shin-shan-shining
    In the bright, blue day.
            —*Walter de la Mare*

"THEN OUT A-SHIN-SHAN-SHINING IN THE BRIGHT BLUE DAY."

THE PARK

I'm glad that I
  Live near a park

For in the winter
  After dark

The park lights shine
  As bright and still

As dandelions
  On a hill.
        —*James S. Tippett*

LAWN-MOWER

I'm the gardener today.
I push the lawn-mower
Across the grass.
  Zwuzz wisssh, zwuzz wisssh.

    I'm the lawn's barber.
    I'm cutting
    Its green hair
      Short.

I push the lawn-mower
Across the grass.
  Zwuzz wisssh.
        —*Dorothy W. Baruch*

SPRINKLING

Sometimes in the summer
When the day is hot
Daddy takes the garden hose
And finds a shady spot;
Then he calls me over
Looks at my bare toes
And says, "Why, you need sprinkling,
You thirsty little rose!"

—*Dorothy Mason Piera*

THE SWING

How do you like to go up in a swing,
　Up in the air so blue?
Oh, I do think it the pleasantest thing
　Ever a child can do!

Up in the air and over the wall,
　Till I can see so wide,
Rivers and trees and cattle and all
　Over the countryside—

Till I look down on the garden green,
　Down on the roof so brown—
Up in the air I go flying again,
　Up in the air and down!

—*Robert Louis Stevenson*

A SWING SONG

Swing, swing,
Sing, sing
Here's my throne, and I am a King!
Swing, sing,
Swing, sing,
Farewell earth, for I'm on the wing!

Low, high,
Here I fly,
Like a bird through sunny sky;
Free, free
Over the lea,
Over the mountain, over the sea!

Up, down,
Up and down,
Which is the way to London Town?
Where, where?
Up in the air,
Close your eyes, and now you are there!

Soon, soon,
Afternoon,
Over the sunset, over the moon;
Far, far
Over all bar,
Sweeping on from star to star!

No, no,
Low, low,
Sweeping daisies with my toe.
Slow, slow,
To and fro,
Slow——— slow——— slow——— s l o w.

—*William Allingham*

DIFFERENT BICYCLES

When I ride my bicycle
I pedal and pedal
Knees up, knees down.
Knees up, knees down.

But when the boy next door
Rides his,
It's whizz—
A chuck a chuck—

And away
He's gone
With his
Knees steady-straight
In one place . . .
Because—
    His bicycle has
    A motor fastened on.
                —*Dorothy W. Baruch*

AT THE SEA-SIDE

When I was down beside the sea
A wooden spade they gave to me
    To dig the sandy shore.

My holes were empty like a cup.
In every hole the sea came up,
    Till it could come no more.
                —*Robert Louis Stevenson*

WINGS AND WHEELS

Ahoy and ahoy, birds!
We cannot have wings
And feathers and things,
But dashing on wheels
With the wind at our heels
Is almost like flying—
Such joy, birds!

Oho and oho, birds!
Of course we can't rise
Up and up to the skies;
But skimming and sliding
On rollers, and gliding,
Is almost as jolly,
You know, birds!

     —*Nancy Byrd Turner*

SHORE

Play on the seashore
And gather up shells,
Kneel in the damp sands
Digging wells.

Run on the rocks
Where the seaweed slips,
Watch the waves
And the beautiful ships.
                    —*Mary Britton Miller*

SKATING

When I try to skate,
My feet are so wary
They grit and they grate:
And then I watch Mary
Easily gliding,
Like an ice-fairy;
Skimming and curving,
Out and in,
With a turn of her head,
And a lift of her chin,
And a gleam of her eye,
And a twirl and a spin;
Sailing under
The breathless hush
Of the willows, and back
To the frozen rush;
Out to the island
And round the edge,
Skirting the rim
Of the crackling sedge,

Swerving close
To the poplar root,
And round the lake
On a single foot,
With a three, and an eight,
And a loop and a ring;
Where Mary glides,
The lake will sing!
Out in the mist
I hear her now
Under the frost
Of the willow-bough
Easily sailing,
Light and fleet,
With the song of the lake
Beneath her feet.

—*Herbert Asquith*

SINGING

Of speckled eggs the birdie sings
   And nests among the trees;
The sailor sings of ropes and things
   In ships upon the seas.

The children sing in far Japan,
   The children sing in Spain;
The organ with the organ man
   Is singing in the rain.

—*Robert Louis Stevenson*

HANDS

There are things
Hands do
That feet never can. Oh
Lots of things
Like stringing beads
Or playing the piano;

Or plaiting little
Stems of grass
Into a little braid
For an acorn
Dolly's head
That somebody has made;

Or shelling slippery
Pods of peas
So the peas can pop;
Or holding things
Quite tightly so
They will not slip or drop.

"Hands, tell my
Toes," I
Said to them one day,
"How you learned
To do so much
More useful things than they."

But hands just
Looked at me
And proudly began:
"Oh, there are things
Hands do
That feet NEVER CAN."

—*Dorothy Aldis*

FEET

There are things
Feet know
That hands never will:
The exciting
Pounding feel
Of running down a hill;

The soft cool
Prickliness
When feet are bare
Walking in
The summer grass
To most anywhere.

Or dabbling in
Water all
Slip-sliddering through toes—
(Nicer than
Through fingers, though why
No one really knows.)

"Toes, tell my
Fingers," I
Said to them one day,
"Why it's such
Fun just to
Wiggle and play."

But toes just
Looked at me
Solemn and still.
Oh, there are things
Feet know
That hands NEVER WILL.

—*Dorothy Aldis*

[47]

THE UMBRELLA BRIGADE

"Pitter patter!" falls the rain
On the school-room window-pane.
Such a plashing! such a dashing!
Will it e'cr be dry again?
Down the gutter rolls a flood,
And the crossing's deep in mud;
And the puddles! oh, the puddles
Are a sight to stir one's blood!

Chorus.   But let it rain
        Tree-toads and frogs,
        Muskets and pitchforks,
        Kittens and dogs!
        Dash away! plash away!
        Who is afraid?
        Here we go,
        The Umbrella Brigade!

Pull the boots up to the knee!
Tie the hoods on merrily!
Such a hustling! such a jostling!
Out of breath with fun are we,
Clatter, clatter, down the street,
Greeting every one we meet,
With our laughing and our chaffing,
Which the laughing drops repeat.

Chorus.   So let it rain
        Tree-toads and frogs,
        Muskets and pitchforks,
        Kittens and dogs!
        Dash away! plash away!
        Who is afraid?
        Here we go,
        The Umbrella Brigade!

—Laura Richards

"ABOUT
AND ROUNDABOUT."

THE MILKMAN

Good luck to the milkman,
He's cold on his cart,
But he whistles a tune
To keep up his heart.
And when we're all sleeping,
Or sleepily drowse,
He's out in the meadows
And milking his cows.

—*Seumas O'Sullivan*

THE MILK-CART PONY

The milk-cart pony in the street
    Is spotted white and brown,
He frisks his mane, he kicks his feet,
    And rattles through the town.

His milk-cans glitter in the sun,
    His harness clinks and rings,
The milk-cart pony on the run
    Must think of lively things.

Perhaps he thinks of circus-tents
    And ladies in top hats,
And orange-peel and sawdust scents,
    And clowns and acrobats.

Perhaps he thinks of Derby Day
    With crowds upon the course
All shouting loud *Hip hip hooray!*
    Here comes the winning horse!

Perhaps he thinks of Dartymoor
    Where he was once a child.
And on the purple-heather floor
    The ponies still run wild.

Well, nobody knows *what* he thinks,
   This little skewbald clown,
Who bears our night and morning drinks
   So noisily through town!
                    —*Eleanor Farjeon*

JIM AT THE CORNER

Jim was a Sailor
Who sailed on the sea.
Now he sits at the corner
From breakfast to tea,
With a nod and a twinkle
For you and for me.

His hair is quite silver,
His eyes are quite blue,
His legs have got pains
So he's nothing to do
But to nod and to twinkle
At me and at you.

He tells all the weather
Without any fuss,
When he says it is thus
Then of *course* it is thus;
He nods as he says it
And twinkles at us.

He knows the world over
From east to west rim,
Now he sits on his box
And the whole world knows Jim.
He nods to the world,
And the world nods to him.
                    —*Eleanor Farjeon*

GENERAL STORE

Some day I'm going to have a store
With a tinkly bell hung over the door,
With real glass cases and counters wide
And drawers all spilly with things inside.
There'll be a little of everything;
Bolts of calico; balls of string;
Jars of peppermint; tins of tea;
Pots and kettles and crockery;
Seeds in packets; scissors bright;
Kegs of sugar, brown and white;
Sarsaparilla for picnic lunches,
Bananas and rubber boots in bunches.
I'll fix the window and dust each shelf,
And take the money in all myself,
It will be my store and I will say:
"What can I do for you to-day?"

—Rachel Field

COUNTERS

To think I once saw grocery shops
   With but a casual eye
And fingered figs and apricots
   As one who came to buy!

To think I never dreamed of how
   Bananas swayed in rain,
And often looked at oranges
   Yet never thought of Spain!

And in those wasted days I saw
   No sails above the tea—
For grocery shops were grocery shops,
   Not hemispheres to me!

—Elizabeth Coatsworth

[53]

THE BALLOON MAN

He always comes on market days,
 And holds balloons—a lovely bunch—
And in the market square he stays,
 And never seems to think of lunch.

They're red and purple, blue and green,
 And when it is a sunny day
Tho' carts and people get between
 You see them shining far away,

And some are big and some are small,
 All tied together with a string,
And if there is a wind at all
 They tug and tug like anything.

Some day perhaps he'll let them go
 And we shall see them sailing high,
And stand and watch them from below—
 They *would* look pretty in the sky!
                              —*Rose Fyleman*

MERRY-GO-ROUND

I climbed up on the merry-go-round,
And it went round and round.

I climbed up on a big brown horse
And it went up and down.

 Around and round
 And up and down,
 Around and round
 And up and down.
 I sat high up
 On a big brown horse

And rode around
On the merry-go-round
And rode around

On the merry-go-round
I rode around
On the merry-go-round
Around
And round
And
Round.
—*Dorothy W. Baruch*

WONDER WHERE THIS HORSESHOE WENT

Wonder where this horseshoe went.
Up and down, up and down.
Up and past the monument,
Maybe into town.

Wait a minute. "Horseshoe,
How far have you been?"
Says it's been to Salem
And halfway to Lynn.

Wonder who was in the team.
Wonder what they saw.
Wonder if they passed a bridge—
Bridge with a draw.

Says it went from one bridge
Straight upon another.
Says it took a little girl
Driving with her mother.
——*Edna St. Vincent Millay*

CIRCUS

The brass band blares,
The naphtha flares,
The sawdust smells,
Showmen ring bells,
And oh! right into the circus-ring
Comes such a lovely, lovely thing,
A milk-white pony with flying tress,
And a beautiful lady,
A beautiful lady,
A *beautiful* lady in a pink dress!
The red-and-white clown
For joy tumbles down,
Like a pink rose
Round she goes
On her tip-toes
With the pony under—
And then, oh, wonder!
The pony his milk-white tresses droops,
And the beautiful lady,
The *beautiful* lady,
Flies like a bird through the paper hoops!
The red-and-white clown for joy falls dead.
Then he waggles his feet and stands on his head,
And the little boys on the twopenny seats
Scream with laughter and suck their sweets.

—*Eleanor Farjeon*

"AND SO HAS A CROCODILE, AND SO
HAS A QUAIL—
THEY'VE ALL GOT TAILS BUT ME!"

THE HAIRY DOG

My dog's so furry I've not seen
His face for years and years:
His eyes are buried out of sight,
I only guess his ears.

When people ask me for his breed,
I do not know or care:
He has the beauty of them all
Hidden beneath his hair.

. .—*Herbert Asquith*

SUNNING

Old Dog lay in the summer sun
Much too lazy to rise and run.
He flapped an ear
At a buzzing fly.
He winked a half opened
Sleepy eye,
He scratched himself
On an itching spot,
As he dozed on the porch
Where the sun was hot.
He whimpered a bit
From force of habit
While he lazily dreamed
Of chasing a rabbit.
But Old Dog happily lay in the sun
Much too lazy to rise and run.

—*James S. Tippett*

RABBITS

My two white rabbits
Chase each other
With humping, bumping backs.
   They go hopping, hopping,
   And their long ears
      Go flopping, flopping.
        And they
        Make faces
        With their noses
        Up and down.

Today
I went inside their fence
To play rabbit with them.
And in one corner
Under a loose bush
I saw something shivering the leaves.
And I pushed
And looked.
And I found—
There
In a hole
In the ground—
Three baby rabbits
Hidden away.
        And *they*
        Made faces
        With their noses
        Up and down.
           —*Dorothy W. Baruch*

THE DRUMMER

Rat-a-tat-tat . . .
See Bunny come
Sporting green breeches
And rolling his drum.

Rat-a-tat-tat . . .
Little pink nose
Must have been snooping
Into a rose.

Rat-a-tat-tat . . .
Rabbit, the drummer,
Straightens his ears
And marches with summer.

—*Anne Robinson*

MEETING THE EASTER BUNNY

On Easter morn at early dawn
   before the cocks were crowing,
I met a bob-tail bunnykin
   and asked where he was going,
" 'Tis in the house and out the house
   a-tipsy, tipsy-toeing,
'Tis round the house and 'bout the house
   a-lightly I am going."
"But what is that of every hue
   you carry in your basket?
" 'Tis eggs of gold and eggs of blue;
   I wonder that you ask it.
'Tis chocolate eggs and bonbon eggs
   and eggs of red and gray,
For every child in every house
   on bonny Easter Day."
He perked his ears and winked his eye
   and twitched his little nose;
He shook his tail—what tail he had—
   and stood up on his toes.
"I must be gone before the sun;
   the East is growing gray;
'Tis almost time for bells to chime."
   So he hippety-hopped away.
          —*Rowena Bastin Bennett*

THE RABBITS' SONG OUTSIDE THE TAVERN

We, who play under the pines,
We, who dance in the snow
That shines blue in the light of the moon,
Sometimes halt as we go—
Stand with our ears erect,
Our noses testing the air,
To gaze at the golden world
Behind the windows there.

Suns they have in a cave,
Stars, each on a tall white stem,
And the thought of a fox or an owl
Seems never to trouble them.
They laugh and eat and are warm,
Their food is ready at hand,
While hungry out in the cold
We little rabbits stand.

But they never dance as we dance!
They haven't the speed nor the grace.
We scorn both the dog and the cat
Who lie by their fireplace.
We scorn them licking their paws
Their eyes on an upraised spoon—
We who dance hungry and wild
Under a winter's moon.

—*Elizabeth Coatsworth*

CAT

My cat
Is quiet
She moves without a sound.
Sometimes she stretches herself
    high and curving
On tiptoe.
Sometimes she crouches low
And creeping.

Sometimes she rubs herself against a chair,
And there
    With a *miew* and a *miew*
    And a purrrr purrrr purrrr
    She curls up
    And goes to sleep.

My cat
Lives through a black hole
Under the house.
So one day I
Crawled in after her.
And it was dark
And I sat
And didn't know
Where to go.
And then—
Two yellow-white
Round little lights
Came moving . . . moving . . . toward me.
And there
With a *miew* and a *miew*
And a purrr purrrr purrrr

My cat
Rubbed, soft, against me.

And I knew
The lights
Were MY CAT'S EYES
In the dark.

—*Dorothy W. Baruch*

CAT

The black cat yawns,
Opens her jaws,
Stretches her legs,
And shows her claws.

Then she gets up
And stands on four
Long stiff legs
And yawns some more.

She shows her sharp teeth,
She stretches her lip,
Her slice of a tongue
Turns up at the tip.

Lifting herself
On her delicate toes,
She arches her back
As high as it goes.

She lets herself down
With particular care,
And pads away
With her tail in the air.

—*Mary Britton Miller*

[65]

DIRGE FOR A RIGHTEOUS KITTEN

Ding-dong, ding-dong, ding-dong.
Here lies a kitten good, who kept
A kitten's proper place.
He stole no pantry eatables.
Nor scratched the baby's face.
He let the alley-cats alone.
He had no yowling vice.
His shirt was always laundried well,
He freed the house of mice.
Until his death he had not caused
His little mistress tears,
He wore his ribbon prettily,
He washed behind his ears.
Ding-dong, ding-dong, ding-dong.
                              —*Vachel Lindsay*

The city mouse lives in a house;—
    The garden mouse lives in a bower,
He's friendly with the frogs and toads,
    And sees the pretty plants in flower.

The city mouse eats bread and cheese;—
    The garden mouse eats what he can;
We will not grudge him seeds and stalks.
    Poor little timid furry man.
                              —*Christina G. Rossetti*

[66]

MICE

I think mice
Are rather nice.

Their tails are long,
Their faces small,
They haven't any
Chins at all.
Their ears are pink,
Their teeth are white,
They run about
The house at night.
They nibble things
They shouldn't touch
And no one seems
To like them much.

But *I* think mice
Are nice.

—Rose Fyleman

THE MOUSE

I heard a mouse
Bitterly complaining
In a crack of moonlight
Aslant on the floor—

"Little I ask
And that little is not granted.
There are few crumbs
In this world any more.

"The bread-box is tin
And I cannot get in.

"The jam's in a jar
My teeth cannot mar.

"The cheese sits by itself
On the pantry shelf—

"All night I run
Searching and seeking,
All night I run
About on the floor.

"Moonlight is there
And a bare place for dancing,
But no little feast
Is spread any more."

—*Elizabeth Coatsworth*

GOOD-MORNING

One day I saw a downy duck,
With feathers on his back;
I said, "Good-morning, downy duck,"
And he said, "Quack, quack, quack."

One day I saw a timid mouse,
He was so shy and meek;
I said, "Good-morning, timid mouse,"
And he said, "Squeak, squeak, squeak."

One day I saw a curly dog,
I met him with a bow;
I said, "Good-morning, curly dog,"
And he said, "Bow-wow-wow."

One day I saw a scarlet bird,
He woke me from my sleep;
I said, "Good-morning, scarlet bird,"
And he said, "Cheep, cheep, cheep."
                              —*Muriel Sipe*

CONVERSATION

I called to gray squirrel,
"Good-day, good-day." . . .
He flirted his tail
In the friendliest way.

I said to red robin,
"Heigh-o, heigh-o." . . .
He stood very straight,
Then bowed very low.

I asked Mistress Tabby,
"Puss, how do you do?"
She purred and she arched,
As she answered, "Mi-eu."

I whistled to Casey,
"Come, hurry, old chap." . . .
How he grinned, how he waggled,
And barked his "Yap . . . yap!" . . .

—Anne Robinson

THE SQUIRREL

Whisky, frisky,
Hippity hop,
Up he goes
To the tree top!

Whirly, twirly,
Round and round,
Down he scampers
To the ground.

Furly, curly
What a tail!
Tall as a feather
Broad as a sail!

Where's his supper?
In the shell,
Snappity, crackity,
Out it fell.

—Author Unknown

D.P.L.

THE ELEPHANT

Here comes the elephant
Swaying along
With his cargo of children
All singing a song:
To the tinkle of laughter
He goes on his way,
And his cargo of children
Have crowned him with may.

His legs are in leather
And padded his toes:
He can root up an oak
With a whisk of his nose:
With a wave of his trunk
And a turn of his chin
He can pull down a house,
Or pick up a pin.

Beneath his gray forehead
A little eye peers;
Of what is he thinking
Between those wide ears?
Of what does he think?
If he wished to tease,
He could twirl his keeper
Over the trees:
If he were not kind,
He could play cup and ball
With Robert and Helen,
And Uncle Paul:
But that gray forehead,
Those crinkled ears,
Have learned to be kind
In a hundred years:

And so with the children
He goes on his way
To the tinkle of laughter
And crowned with the may.
                    —*Herbert Asquith*

NATURE NOTE

Undoubtedly the Kangaroos
    Have fun;
They hop because they do not choose
    To run.
                    —*Arthur Guiterman*

THE LITTLE TURTLE

There was a little turtle.
He lived in a box.
He swam in a puddle.
He climbed on the rocks.

He snapped at a mosquito.
He snapped at a flea.
He snapped at a minnow.
And he snapped at me.

He caught the mosquito.
He caught the flea.
He caught the minnow.
But he didn't catch me.

—*Vachel Lindsay*

"ALL TO THE HAVEN
WHERE EACH WOULD BE,
FLY!"

Fuzzy wuzzy, creepy crawly
    Caterpillar funny,
You will be a butterfly
    When the days are sunny.

Winging, flinging, dancing, springing
    Butterfly so yellow,
You were once a caterpillar,
    Wiggly, wiggly fellow.
                              —*Lillian Schulz*

Brown and furry
Caterpillar in a hurry
Take your walk
To the shady leaf, or stalk,
Or what not,
Which may be the chosen spot.
No toad spy you,
Hovering bird of prey pass by you:
Spin and die,
To live again a butterfly.
                —*Christina G. Rossetti*

ENVOI

Fly, white butterflies, out to sea,
Frail pale wings for the wind to try,
Small white wings that we scarce can see,
    Fly.

Some fly light as a laugh of glee,
Some fly soft as a low long sigh:
All to the haven where each would be,
    Fly.
        —Algernon Charles Swinburne

DOWN IN THE HOLLOW

Down in the hollow,
Not so far away,
I saw a little ladybug
When I went to play,

Swinging on the clover
Up in the air . . .
I wonder if the ladybug
Knew that I was there.
        —Aileen Fisher

HONEY BEE

Honey bee, honey bee! here is some money;
Take it and bring us a pot of new honey!
Fly away! fly, you buzzing old rover!
Gather us sweets from the blossoming clover.
        —Lucy Fitch Perkins

[78]

FIREFLY
A Song

A little light is going by,
Is going up to see the sky,
A little light with wings.

I never could have thought of it,
To have a little bug all lit
And made to go on wings.

—*Elizabeth Madox Roberts*

THE BLACKBIRD

In the far corner
close by the swings,
every morning
a blackbird sings.

His bill's so yellow,
his coat's so black,
that he makes a fellow
whistle back.

Ann, my daughter,
thinks that he
sings for us two
especially.

—*Humbert Wolfe*

Wrens and robins in the hedge,
  Wrens and robins here and there;
Building, perching, pecking, fluttering,
  Everywhere!
                    —*Christina G. Rossetti*

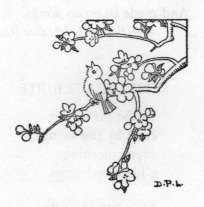

Be like the bird, who
Halting in his flight
On limb too slight
Feels it give way beneath him,
Yet sings
Knowing he hath wings.
                    —*Victor Hugo*

THE SONG OF THE ROBIN

The cows low in the pasture on the hill,
The bluebird sings, building a nest,
The water is singing down by the mill—
But the robin's song is the best!

The squirrels are chattering in the trees,
The wind is blowing toward the west,
Around the flowers are humming bees—
But the robin's song is the best!

The dogwood trees are blossoming white,
The plow horse is neighing for rest,
The song sparrow is singing with all his might—
But the robin's song is the best!

—Beatrice Bergquist

HERONS

A breeze blows o'er the lake;
Against the heron's slender legs
The little ripples break.

If they had no voices, lo!
White herons would be
But a line of snow.

—Japanese Hokku

THE EAGLE

Fragment

He clasps the crag with hooked hands;
Close to the sun in lonely lands,
Ring'd with the azure world, he stands,

The wrinkled sea beneath him crawls;
He watches from his mountain walls,
And like a thunderbolt he falls.

—*Alfred Tennyson*

SONG—THE OWL

When cats run home and light is come,
    And dew is cold upon the ground,
And the far-off stream is dumb,
    And the whirring sail goes round,
    And the whirring sail goes round;
        Alone and warming his five wits,
        The white owl in the belfry sits.
When merry milkmaids click the latch,
    And rarely smells the new-mown hay,
And the cock hath sung beneath the thatch
    Twice or thrice his roundelay,
    Twice or thrice his roundelay;
        Alone and warming his five wits,
        The white owl in the belfry sits.

—*Alfred Tennyson*

"LAUGHING WITH FRIENDS,
I'M ALWAYS SORRY
WHEN THE RIDE ENDS."

STOP—GO

Automobiles
In
  a
    row
Wait to go
While the signal says:
                    STOP

Bells ring
Tingaling
Red light's gone!
Green light's on!
Horns blow!
And the row
Starts
          to
                GO
      —*Dorothy W. Baruch*

ENGINE

I wonder if the engine
That dashes down the track
Ever has a single thought
Of how it can get back.

With fifty cars behind it
And each car loaded full,
I wonder if it ever thinks
How hard it has to pull.

I guess it trusts the fireman;
It trusts the engineer;
I guess it knows the switchman
Will keep the tracks clear.
          —*James S. Tippett*

[85]

TRAINS

Over the mountains
Over the plains,
Over the rivers,
Here come the trains.

Carrying passengers,
Carrying mail,
Bringing their precious loads
In without fail.

Thousands of freight cars
All rushing on
Through day and darkness
Through dusk and dawn.

Over the mountains,
Over the plains,
Over the rivers,
Here come the trains.

—*James S. Tippett*

A LETTER IS A GYPSY ELF

A letter is a gypsy elf
It goes where I would go myself:
East or West or North, it goes,
Or South past pretty bungalows,
Over mountain, over hill,
Any place it must and will,
It finds good friends that live so far
You cannot travel where they are.

—*Annette Wynne*

THE ELEVATED TRAIN

Great, creaking worm
On a skeleton's back,
Screech when you grind
Your round feet on its track.

Sometimes I watch you
Slip on through the city,
Shaking the shivering bones
Without pity.

Ever more silent,
Far down the street
You lose yourself
Where the tall buildings meet.
—*James S. Tippett*

FERRY-BOATS

Over the river,
Over the bay,
Ferry-boats travel
Every day.

Most of the people
Crowd to the side
Just to enjoy
Their ferry-boat ride.

Watching the seagulls,
Laughing with friends,
I'm always sorry
When the ride ends.
—*James S. Tippett*

UP IN THE AIR

Zooming across the sky,
Like a great bird you fly.
Airplane,
Silvery white
In the light.

Turning and twisting in air,
When shall I ever be there.
Airplane,
Piloting you
Far in the blue?
—*James S. Tippett*

"Ferry me across the water,
Do, boatman, do."
"If you've a penny in your purse
I'll ferry you."

"I have a penny in my purse,
And my eyes are blue;
So ferry me across the water,
Do, boatman, do!"

"Step into my ferry-boat,
Be they black or blue,
And for the penny in your purse
I'll ferry you."
—*Christina G. Rossetti*

In the evening from my window
    Just before I go to bed
I can watch the trains a-gliding
    Beneath the stars that shine o'erhead.
Far away, the engine seems a beetle black
Drawing lines of flowing fireflies on a track.

How I wonder where they are going,
    What they will see before the day,
Mighty mountains, lonely forests,
    Sleeping cities far away.
Arching bridges, long, long trestles
    They'll pass o'er
Plunging into darksome tunnels with a roar.
                        —*Author Unknown*

MY SHIP AND I

O it's I that am the captain of a tidy little ship,
    Of a ship that goes a-sailing on the pond;
And my ship it keeps a-turning all around and all about;
But when I'm a little older, I shall find the secret out
    How to send my vessel sailing on beyond.

For I mean to grow as little as the dolly at the helm,
    And the dolly I intend to come alive;
And with him beside to help me, it's a-sailing I shall go,
It's a-sailing on the water, when the jolly breezes blow
    And the vessel goes a divie-divie-dive.

O it's then you'll see me sailing through the rushes and
        reeds.
    And you'll hear the water singing at the prow;
For besides the dolly sailor, I'm to voyage and explore,
To land upon the island where no dolly was before,
    And to fire the penny cannon in the bow.
                        —*Robert Louis Stevenson*

[89]

WHERE GO THE BOATS

Dark brown is the river,
 Golden is the sand.
It flows along for ever,
 With trees on either hand.

Green leaves a-floating,
 Castles of the foam,
Boats of mine a-boating—
 Where will all come home?

On goes the river
 And out past the mill,
Away down the valley,
 Away down the hill.

Away down the river,
 A hundred miles or more,
Other little children
 Shall bring my boats ashore.
 —*Robert Louis Stevenson*

"MINNIE AND MATTIE
    AND FAT LITTLE MAY,
OUT IN THE COUNTRY,
    SPENDING A DAY."

Minnie and Mattie
  And fat little May,
Out in the country,
  Spending a day.

Such a bright day,
  With the sun glowing,
And the trees half in leaf,
  And the grass growing.

Pinky white pigling
  Squeals through his snout,
Woolly white lambkin
  Frisks all about,

Cluck! cluck! the nursing hen
  Summons her folk,—
Ducklings all downy soft,
  Yellow as yolk.

Cluck! cluck! the mother hen
  Summons her chickens
To peck the dainty bits
  Found in her pickings.

Minnie and Mattie
  And May carry posies,
Half of sweet violets,
  Half of primroses.
          —*Christina G. Rossetti*

FAMILIAR FRIENDS

The horses, the pigs,
And the chickens,
The turkeys, the ducks
And the sheep!
I can see all my friends
From my window
As soon as I waken
From sleep.

The cat on the fence
Is out walking.
The geese have gone down
For a swim.
The pony comes trotting
Right up to the gate;
He knows I have candy
For him.

The cows in the pasture
Are switching
Their tails to keep off
The flies.
And the old mother dog
Has come out in the yard
With five pups to give me
A surprise.

—James S. Tippett

THE HENS

The night was coming very fast;
It reached the gate as I ran past.

The pigeons had gone to the tower of the church
And all the hens were on their perch,

Up in the barn, and I thought I heard
A piece of a little purring word.

I stopped inside, waiting and staying,
To try to hear what the hens were saying.

They were asking something, that was plain,
Asking it over and over again.

One of them moved and turned around,
Her feathers made a ruffled sound,

A ruffled sound, like a bushful of birds,
And she said her little asking words.

She pushed her head close into her wing,
But nothing answered anything.
                    —Elizabeth Madox Roberts

MRS. PECK-PIGEON

Mrs. Peck-Pigeon
Is picking for bread,
Bob-bob-bob
Goes her little round head.
Tame as a pussy-cat
In the street,
Step-step-step
Go her little red feet.
With her little red feet
And her little round head,
Mrs. Peck-Pigeon
Goes picking for bread.
                    —Eleanor Farjeon

DUCK'S DITTY

All along the backwater,
Through the rushes tall,
Ducks are a-dabbling,
Up tails all!

Ducks' tails, drakes' tails,
Yellow feet a-quiver,
Yellow bills all out of sight
Busy in the river!

Slushy green undergrowth
Where the roach swim—
Here we keep our larder,
Cool and full and dim!

Every one for what he likes!
We like to be
Heads down, tails up,
Dabbling free!

High in the blue above
Swifts whirl and call—
We are down a-dabbling
Up tails all!

Kenneth Grahame

THE BUTTERBEAN TENT

All through the garden I went and went,
And I walked in under the butterbean tent.

The poles leaned up like a good tepee
And made a nice little house for me.

I had a hard brown clod for a seat,
And all outside was a cool green street.

A little green worm and a butterfly
And a cricket-like thing that could hop went by.

Hidden away there were flocks and flocks
Of bugs that could go like little clocks.

Such a good day it was when I spent
A long, long while in the butterbean tent.
                    —*Elizabeth Madox Roberts*

THE CORNFIELD

I went across the pasture lot
When not a one was watching me.
Away beyond the cattle barns
I climbed a little crooked tree.

And I could look down on the field
And see the corn and how it grows
Across the world and up and down
In very straight and even rows.

And far away and far away—
I wonder if the farmer man
Knows all about the corn and how
It comes together like a fan.
                    —*Elizabeth Madox Roberts*

[97]

THE SCARECROW

A scarecrow stood in a field one day,
  Stuffed with straw,
  Stuffed with hay;
He watched the folk on the king's highway,
  But never a word said he.

Much he saw but naught did heed,
  Knowing not night,
  Knowing not day,
For having naught, did nothing heed
  And never a word said he.

A little grey mouse had made its nest,
  Oh so wee,
  Oh so grey,
In a sleeve of a coat that was poor Tom's best,
  But the scarecrow naught said he.

His hat was the home of a small jenny wren,
  Ever so sweet,
  Ever so gay,
A squirrel had put by his fear of men,
  And hissed him, but naught heeded he.

Ragged old man, I loved him well,
  Stuffed with straw,
  Stuffed with hay,
Many's the tale that he could tell,
  But never a word says he.

—*Michael Franklin*

MILKING TIME

When supper time is almost come,
But not quite here, I cannot wait,
And so I take my china mug
And go down by the milking gate.

The cow is always eating shucks
And spilling off the little silk.
Her purple eyes are big and soft—
She always smells like milk.

And Father takes my mug from me,
And then he makes the stream come out.
I see it going in my mug
And foaming all about.

And when it's piling very high,
And when some little streams commence
To run and drip along the sides,
He hands it to me through the fence.
                    —*Elizabeth Madox Roberts*

THE PASTURE

I'm going out to clean the pasture spring;
I'll only stop to rake the leaves away
(And wait to watch the water clear, I may):
I sha'n't be gone long.—You come too.

I'm going out to fetch the little calf
That's standing by the mother. It's so young,
It totters when she licks it with her tongue.
I sha'n't be gone long.—You come too.
                    —*Robert Frost*

[99]

THE COW

The friendly cow all red and white,
    I love with all my heart:
She gives me cream, with all her might,
    To eat with apple-tart.

She wanders lowing here and there,
    And yet she cannot stray,
All in the pleasant open air,
    The pleasant light of day:

And blown by all the winds that pass
    And wet with all the showers,
She walks among the meadow grass
    And eats the meadow flowers.
            —Robert Louis Stevenson

COLTS

Colts behind their mothers
Trot across the plain,
Rustling, zoro-zoro, like a lady's
train.
—*Japanese Hokku*

The horses of the sea
Rear a foaming crest,
But the horses of the land
Serve us best.

The horses of the land
Munch corn and clover,
While the foaming sea-horses
Toss and turn over.
—*Christina G. Rossetti*

THE LAMB

Little lamb, who made thee?
Dost thou know who made thee?
Gave thee life, and bid thee feed
By the stream and o'er the mead;
Gave thee clothing of delight,
Softest clothing, woolly, bright;
Gave thee such a tender voice,
Making all the vales rejoice?
Little lamb, who made thee?
Dost thou know who made thee?

Little lamb, I'll tell thee;
Little lamb, I'll tell thee;
He is calléd by thy name,
For He calls Himself a Lamb.
He is meek, and he is mild,
He became a little child,
I a child, and thou a lamb
We are calléd by his name.
Little lamb, God bless thee!
Little lamb, God bless thee!
—*William Blake*

"AWAKE! OH, NORTH WIND,
AND COME, THOU SOUTH,
BLOW YOU UPON MY GARDEN."

Awake! Oh, North Wind,
And come, thou South,
Blow you upon my garden.
                —*Song of Solomon* iv. 16

LILIES

I thought I saw white clouds, but no!—
Bending across the fence,
White lilies in a row!
                —*Shiko* 1665–1731

THE RAINS OF SPRING

The rains of spring
Which hang to the branches
Of the green willow,
Look like pearls upon a string.
                —*Lady Ise* about 1000 A.D.

NAMES

Larkspur and Hollyhock,
Pink Rose and purple Stock,
Lovely smelling Mignonette,
Lilies not quite opened yet,
Phlox the favorite of bees,
Bleeding Heart and Peonies—
Just their names are nice to say,
Softly,
On a summer's day.
                —*Dorothy Aldis*

What is pink? a rose is pink
By the fountain's brink.
What is red? a poppy's red
In its barley bed.
What is blue? the sky is blue
Where the clouds float thro'.
What is white? a swan is white
Sailing in the light.
What is yellow? pears are yellow,
Rich and ripe and mellow.
What is green? the grass is green,
With small flowers between.
What is violet? clouds are violet
In the summer twilight.
What is orange? why, an orange,
Just an orange!
                         —*Christina G. Rossetti*

PLUM BLOSSOMS

Far across hill and dale
The blossoms of the plum have cast
A delicate pink veil.

                         —*Bashō*

So sweet the plum trees smell!
Would that the brush that paints the flower
Could paint the scent as well.

                         —*Japanese Hokku*

I came to look, and lo,
The plum tree petals scatter down
A fall of purest snow.

                         —*Reinkō* 1728-99

DAFFODILS

In spite of cold and chills
That usher in the early spring,
We have the daffodils.
—*Japanese Hokku*

CHILD'S SONG

I have a garden of my own,
   Shining with flow'rs of ev'ry hue;
I loved it dearly while alone,
   But I shall love it more with you:
And there the golden bees shall come,
   In summer-time at break of morn,
And wake us with their busy hum
   Around the Siha's fragrant thorn.

I have a fawn from Aden's land,
   On leafy buds and berries nurst,
And you shall feed him from your hand,
   Though he may start with fear at first.
And I will lead you where he lies
   For shelter in the noontide heat;
And you may touch his sleeping eyes,
   And feel his little silv'ry feet.
—*Thomas Moore*

OUTSIDE THE DOOR

Outside the door the bare tree stands,
And catches snowflakes in its hands,
And holds them well and holds them high,
Until a puffing wind comes by.

—*Annette Wynne*

THE LITTLE ROSE TREE

Every rose on the little tree
Is making a different face at me!

Some look surprised when I pass by,
And others droop—but they are shy.

These two whose heads together press
Tell secrets I could never guess.

Some have their heads thrown back to sing,
And all the buds are listening.

I wonder if the gardener knows,
Or if he calls each just a rose?

—*Rachel Field*

THE SNAIL

The snail is very odd and slow.
He has his mind made up to go
The longest way to anywhere
And will not let you steer him there.

Today I met one in the grass
And hadn't time to watch him pass,
But coming back at sunset, I
Discovered him still traveling by.

The grass-blades grew so thick and tall
I asked him why he climbed them all,
And told him I had sometimes found
The shortest way was going 'round.

He was not easy to persuade,
To judge by any sign he made,
And when I lectured him some more
Went in his house and shut the door.

—Grace Hazard Conkling

THE TREE STANDS VERY STRAIGHT
AND STILL

The tree stands very straight and still
All night long far on the hill;
But if I go and listen near
A million little sounds I hear,
The leaves are little whispering elves
Talking, playing by themselves,
Playing softly altogether
In the warm or windy weather,
Talking softly to the sky
Or any bird that dartles by,
O little elves within the tree,
Is there no word to tell to me?

—Annette Wynne

STOPPING BY WOODS ON A
SNOWY EVENING

Whose woods these are I think I know.
His house is in the village though;
He will not see me stopping here
To watch his woods fill up with snow.

The little horse must think it queer
To stop without a farmhouse near
Between the woods and frozen lake
The darkest evening of the year.

He gives his harness bells a shake
To ask if there is some mistake.
The only other sound's the sweep
Of easy wind and downy flake.

The woods are lovely, dark and deep.
But I have promises to keep,
And miles to go before I sleep,
And miles to go before I sleep.
                    —*Robert Frost*

Come ride and ride to the garden,
    Come ride and ride with a will:
For the flower comes with the fruit there
    Beyond a hill and a hill.

    Refrain. Come ride and ride to the garden,
            Come ride like the March wind;
        There's barley there, and water there,
            And stabling to your mind.

O scent of the broken apples!
    O shuffling of holy shoes!
Beyond a hill and a hill there
    In the land that no one knows.

    Refrain. Come ride and ride to the garden,
            Come ride like the March wind;
        There's barley there, and water there,
            And stabling to your mind.
                    —*Lady Gregory*
                    The Travelling Man

LAUGHING SONG

When the green woods laugh with the voice of joy,
And the dimpling stream runs laughing by;
When the air does laugh with our merry wit,
And the green hill laughs with the noise of it;

When the meadows laugh with lively green,
And the grasshopper laughs in the merry scene,
When Mary and Susan and Emily
With their sweet round mouth sing "Ha, Ha, He!"

When the painted birds laugh in the shade,
Where our table with cherries and nuts is spread,
Come live and be merry, and join with me,
To sing the sweet chorus of "Ha, Ha, He!"

—*William Blake*

"SUPPOSE—
AND SUPPOSE."

THE HORSEMAN

I heard a horseman
  Ride over the hill;
The moon shone clear,
  The night was still;
His helm was silver,
  And pale was he;
And the horse he rode
  Was of ivory.
      —*Walter de la Mare*

SOME ONE

Some one came knocking
  At my wee, small door;
Some one came knocking,
  I'm sure—sure—sure;
I listened, I opened,
  I looked to left and right,
But nought there was a-stirring
  In the still dark night;
Only the busy beetle
  Tap-tapping in the wall,
Only from the forest
  The screech-owl's call,
Only the cricket whistling
  While the dewdrops fall,
So I know not who came knocking,
  At all, at all, at all.
      —*Walter de la Mare*

THE WIND AND THE MOON

Said the Wind to the Moon,
"I will blow you out;
    You stare
    In the air
    Like a ghost in a chair
Always looking what I am about.
I hate to be watched—I'll blow you
        out."

—*George MacDonald*

WHITE HORSES

Little white horses are out on the sea,
    Bridled with rainbows and speckled with foam,
Laden with presents for you and for me;
    Mermaids and fairies are riding them home!
                    Gold from the sun;
                    Diamonds rare
                    Made from dew
                    And frosty air;
                    Veils of mist,
                    Soft and white,
                    Rose and silver,
                    Shimmering, bright;
                    Sweetest perfumes,
                    Coloured shells,
                    Lilting music,
                    Fairy bells:
Fairies and mermaids are bringing them home
On Little White Horses all speckled with foam.
                    —*Winifred Howard*

OTHERWISE

There must be magic,
Otherwise,
How could day turn to night,

And how could sailboats,
Otherwise,
Go sailing out of sight,

And how could peanuts,
Otherwise,
Be covered up so tight?
                    —*Aileen Fisher*

[117]

I saw the wind to-day:
I saw it in the pane
Of glass upon the wall:
A moving thing,—'twas like
No bird with widening wing,
No mouse that runs along
The meal bag under the beam.

I think it like a horse,
All black, with frightening mane,
That springs out of the earth,
And tramples on his way.
I saw it in the glass,
The shaking of a mane:
A horse that no one rides!
                              —*Padraic Colum*

THE WEATHER FACTORY

Just as soon as summer's done,
Such a flit and flutter!
In the weather factory
Such a clip-and-clutter!

Nuts are begging, "Send us frost!"
In a month or so,
Children will be saying, "Ah,
If 'twould only snow!"

So the little weather folk
Dash around and scurry;
Everybody with a job,
Working in a flurry.

"Winkle, Twinkle, mix the frost.
Hoppy, grind the hail.
Make icicles, Nip and Tuck—
Thousands, without fail!

Tippy, start the flake machine
Quickly, and remember—
Twenty million tons of snow
Needed by November.

Whipper, Snapper, hurry up!"
Soon as autumn's come,
In the weather factory
Things begin to hum.
                    —*Nancy Byrd Turner*

THE POTATOES' DANCE

I

"Down cellar," said the cricket,
"Down cellar," said the cricket,
"Down cellar," said the cricket,
"I saw a ball last night,
In honor of a lady,
In honor of a lady,
In honor of a lady,
Whose wings were pearly white.
The breath of bitter weather,
The breath of bitter weather,
The breath of bitter weather,
Had smashed the cellar pane.
We entertained a drift of leaves,
We entertained a drift of leaves,
We entertained a drift of leaves,
And then of snow and rain.
But we were dressed for winter,
But we were dressed for winter,
But we were dressed for winter,
And loved to hear it blow.
In honor of the lady,
In honor of the lady,
In honor of the lady,
Who makes potatoes grow,
Our guest the Irish lady,
The tiny Irish lady,
The airy Irish lady,
Who makes potatoes grow.

II

"Potatoes were the waiters,
Potatoes were the waiters,
Potatoes were the waiters,
Potatoes were the band,
Potatoes were the dancers
Kicking up the sand,
Kicking up the sand,
Kicking up the sand,
Potatoes were the dancers
Kicking up the sand.
Their legs were old burnt matches,
Their legs were old burnt matches,
Their legs were old burnt matches,
Their arms were just the same.
They jigged and whirled and scrambled,
Jigged and whirled and scrambled,
Jigged and whirled and scrambled,
In honor of the dame,
The noble Irish lady
Who makes potatoes dance,
The witty Irish lady,
The saucy Irish lady
The laughing Irish lady
Who makes potatoes prance.

III

"There was just one sweet potato
He was golden brown and slim.
The lady loved his dancing,
The lady loved his dancing,
The lady loved his dancing,
She danced all night with him,
She danced all night with him.

Alas, he wasn't Irish
So when she flew away,
They threw him in the coal-bin,
And there he is today,
Where they cannot hear his sighs
And his weeping for the lady,
The glorious Irish lady,
The beauteous Irish lady,
Who
Gives
Potatoes
Eyes."

—Vachel Lindsay

"WEE FOLK, GOOD FOLK
TROOPING ALL TOGETHER.."

THE LIGHT-HEARTED FAIRY

Oh, who is so merry, so merry, heigh ho!
As the light-hearted fairy? heigh ho,
    Heigh ho!
  He dances and sings
  To the sound of his wings,
With a hey and a heigh and a ho!

Oh, who is so merry, so airy, heigh ho!
As the light-hearted fairy? heigh ho,
    Heigh ho!
  His nectar he sips
  From the primroses' lips
With a hey and a heigh and a ho!

Oh, who is so merry, so merry, heigh ho!
As the light-hearted fairy? heigh ho!
    Heigh ho!
  The night is his noon
  And his sun is the moon,
With a hey and a heigh and a ho!
              —*Author Unknown*

ONCE WHEN YOU WERE WALKING

Once when you were walking across the
    meadow grass,
A little fairy touched you—but you
    never saw her pass.

One day when you were sitting upon a
    mossy stone,
A fairy sat beside you, but you thought
    you were alone.

So no matter what you do, no matter
    where you go,
A fairy may be near you—but you may
    never know.

—*Annette Wynne*

A FAIRY WENT A-MARKETING

A fairy went a-marketing—
    She bought a little fish;
She put it in a crystal bowl
    Upon a golden dish.
An hour she sat in wonderment
    And watched its silver gleam,
And then she gently took it up
    And slipped it in a stream.

A fairy went a-marketing—
　　She bought a coloured bird;
It sang the sweetest, shrillest song
　　That ever she had heard.
She sat beside its painted cage
　　And listened half the day,
And then she opened wide the door
　　And let it fly away.

A fairy went a-marketing—
　　She bought a winter gown
All stitched about with gossamer
　　And lined with thistledown.
She wore it all the afternoon
　　With prancing and delight,
Then gave it to a little frog
　　To keep him warm at night.

A fairy went a-marketing—
　　She bought a gentle mouse
To take her tiny messages,
　　To keep her tiny house.
All day she kept its busy feet
　　Pit-patting to and fro,
And then she kissed its silken ears,
　　Thanked it, and let it go.
　　　　　　　　　—*Rose Fyleman*

FAIRY WINGS

Through the windmills
Fairies weave
Stuff for wings
From the breath
Of the winds
On the hills.

From the South
Comes the blue;
From the West
Saffron hue;
From the East
Comes the rose,
And the North
Brings the silver
From the snows.

Colours blended,
Dainty, fair;
Silken fabric
Light as air.

They fashion as wings,
And spread them to catch
The sunshine at noon;
Dip into dew,
And hang them to dry,
On a clear frosty night,
From the beams of the moon.
—*Winifred Howard*

IN THE MOONLIGHT

The Fairies dance the livelong night
Across the moonlit hill;
The moonbeams dance along the lake;
The western wind is still.
The waters make a little sound
More sweet than music far—
Oh, let me fly across the world
To where the Fairies are!

—*Norreys Jepson O'Conor*

MR. MOON
A Song of the Little People

O Moon, Mr. Moon,
When you comin' down?
Down on the hilltop,
Down in the glen,
Out in the clearin',
To play with little men?
Moon, Mr. Moon,
When you comin' down?

O Mr. Moon,
Hurry up along!
The reeds in the current
Are whisperin' slow;
The river's a-wimplin'
To and fro.
Hurry up along,
Or you'll miss the song!
Moon, Mr. Moon,
When you comin' down?

O Moon, Mr. Moon,
When you comin' down?
Down where the Good Folk
Dance in a ring,
Down where the Little Folk
Sing?
Moon, Mr. Moon,
When you comin' down?
—*Bliss Carman*

THE FAIRIES

Up the airy mountain,
  Down the rushy glen,
We daren't go a-hunting
  For fear of little men;
Wee folk, good folk,
  Trooping all together;
Green jacket, red cap,
  And white owl's feather!

Down along the rocky shore
  Some make their home,
They live on crispy pancakes
  Of yellow tide-foam;
Some in the reeds
  Of the black mountain-lake,
With frogs for their watch-dogs,
  All night awake.

High on the hill-top
   The old King sits;
He is now so old and gray
   He's nigh lost his wits.
With a bridge of white mist
   Columbkill he crosses
On his stately journeys
   From Slieveleague to Rosses;
Or going up with music
   On cold, starry nights,
To sup with the Queen
   Of the gay Northern Lights.

They stole little Bridget
   For seven years long;
When she came down again
   Her friends were all gone.
They took her lightly back,
   Between the night and morrow;
They thought that she was fast asleep,
   But she was dead with sorrow.
They have kept her ever since
   Deep within the lake,
On a bed of flag-leaves,
   Watching till she wake.

By the craggy hill-side,
   Through the mosses bare,
They have planted thorn-trees
   For pleasure here and there.
Is any man so daring
   As to dig them up in spite,
He shall find their sharpest thorns
   In his bed at night.

Up the airy mountain,
   Down the rushy glen,
We daren't go a-hunting
   For fear of little men;
Wee folk, good folk,
   Trooping all together;
Green jacket, red cap,
   And white owl's feather.
                    —*William Allingham*

TWENTY FOOLISH FAIRIES

Somebody left a mirror
   Out on the lawn last night,
And twenty foolish fairies,
In the dim moonlight,
Mistook it for an ice-pond,
When the morning broke
Twenty early robins
Chuckled at the joke.
                    —*Nancy Byrd Turner*

"WHERE WE WALK TO SCHOOL EACH DAY
INDIAN CHILDREN USED TO PLAY."

INDIAN CHILDREN

Where we walk to school each day
Indian children used to play—
All about our native land,
Where the shops and houses stand.

And the trees were very tall,
And there were no streets at all,
Not a church and not a steeple—
Only woods and Indian people.

Only wigwams on the ground,
And at night bears prowling round—
What a different place to-day
Where we live and work and play!

—*Annette Wynne*

INDIAN PIPE AND MOCCASIN FLOWER

Indian pipe and moccasin flower
  Grow where the woodland waves,
Grow in the moss and the bracken bower
  Trod by the light-foot braves
Who played their part, who lived their hour
  And left, with a name that thrills,
Indian pipe and moccasin flower
  Scattered among our hills.

—*Arthur Guiterman*

LULLABY
Hopi Indians

Puva ... puva ... puva,
In the trail the beetles
On each other's backs are sleeping,
So on mine, my baby, thou.
Puva ... puva ... puva.
                    —*Trans. by Natalie Curtis*

WIND-SONG
Pima Indians
(Medicine Song)

Far on the desert ridges
  Stands the cactus;
Lo, the blossoms swaying
To and fro, the blossoms swaying, swaying.
                    —*Trans. by Natalie Curtis*

THE LOCUST

Locust, locust, playing a flute,
Locust, locust, playing a flute!
Away up above on the pine-tree bough,
Closely clinging,
            Playing a flute,
            Playing a flute!
            —*Trans. by Frank Cushing*

CORN-GRINDING SONG
Zuñi Indians

Yonder, yonder see the fair rainbow,
See the rainbow brightly decked and painted!
Now the swallow bringeth glad news to your corn,
Singing, "Hitherward, hitherward, hitherward, rain,
    Hither, come!"
Singing, "Hitherward, hitherward, hitherward, white
      cloud,
    Hither, come!"
Now hear the corn-plants murmur,
"We are growing everywhere!
Hi, yai! The world, how fair!"

                   —*Trans. by Natalie Curtis*

CORN-GRINDING SONG
Laguna Indians

Butterflies, butterflies,
Now fly away to the blossoms,
Fly blue-wing,
Fly yellow-wing,
Now fly away to the blossoms,
Fly red-wing,
Fly white-wing,
Now fly away to the blossoms,
Butterflies, away!
Butterflies, butterflies,
Now fly away to the blossoms,
Butterflies, away!
—*Trans. by Natalie Curtis*

"COME, CHOOSE YOUR ROAD AND AWAY!"

FOREIGN LANDS

Up into the cherry tree
Who should climb but little me?
I held the trunk with both my hands
And looked abroad on foreign lands.

I saw the next door garden lie,
Adorned with flowers, before my eye,
And many pleasant places more
That I had never seen before.

I saw the dimpling river pass
And be the sky's blue looking-glass;
The dusty roads go up and down
With people tramping in to town.

If I could find a higher tree
Farther and farther I should see,
To where the grown-up river slips
Into the sea among the ships.

To where the roads on either hand
Lead onward into fairy land,
Where all the children dine at five,
And all the playthings come alive.

—*Robert Louis Stevenson*

THE UNEXPLORER

There was a road ran past our house
Too lovely to explore.
I asked my mother once—she said
That if you followed where it led
It brought you to a milk-man's door.
(That's why I have not traveled more.)
                    —*Edna St. Vincent Millay*

BABY TOES

There is a blue star, Janet,
Fifteen years' ride from us,
If we ride a hundred miles an hour.

There is a white star, Janet,
Forty years' ride from us,
If we ride a hundred miles an hour.

Shall we ride
To the blue star
Or the white star?
                    —*Carl Sandburg*

CALLED AWAY

I meant to do my work today—
But a brown bird sang in the apple tree,
And a butterfly flitted across the field,
And all the leaves were calling me.

And the wind went sighing over the land
Tossing the grasses to and fro,
And a rainbow held out its shining hand—
So what could I do but laugh and go?

—Richard Le Gallienne

SHIPS

Go out, good ships, across the tide,
Be brave to meet all weathers;
Make many a port, and fill each hold
With sky-blue silk and yellow gold
And pearls and peacock feathers.

The wind is in your shining sails,
Your keen prows cut the foam;
Sail very fast and very far,
Then turn, and by the Northern Star
Come steering safely home.

—*Nancy Byrd Turner*

THE CALL OF THE SPRING
(Refrain)

Come, choose your road and away, my lad,
Come, choose your road and away!
We'll out of the town by the road's bright crown
As it dips to the sapphire day.
All roads may meet at the world's end,
But, hey for the heart of May!
Come, choose your road and away, dear lad,
Come, choose your road and away.

—*Alfred Noyes*

"AND EVERYTHING THAT'S MINE
IS YOURS, AND YOURS, AND YOURS."

A SHOWER

Shower came;
In I came;
Blue sky came!

                    —*Izembo. d. 1710*

RAIN

The rain is raining all around,
    It falls on field and tree,
It rains on the umbrellas here,
    And on the ships at sea.
            —*Robert Louis Stevenson*

APRIL RAIN SONG

Let the rain kiss you.
Let the rain beat upon your head with silver liquid drops.
Let the rain sing you a lullaby.

The rain makes still pools on the sidewalk.
The rain makes running pools in the gutter.
The rain plays a little sleep-song on our roof at night—

And I love the rain.

                    . .—*Langston Hughes*

LITTLE WIND

Little wind, blow on the hill-top;
Little wind, blow down the plain;
Little wind, blow up the sunshine,
Little wind, blow off the rain.
                —*Kate Greenaway*

[147]

LITTLE RAIN

When I was making myself a game
Up in the garden, a little rain came.

It fell down quick in a sort of rush,
And I crawled back under the snowball bush.

I could hear the big drops hit the ground
And see little puddles of dust fly round.

A chicken came till the rain was gone;
He had just a very few feathers on.

He shivered a little under his skin,
And then he shut his eyeballs in.

Even after the rain had begun to hush
It kept on raining up in the bush.

One big flat drop came sliding down,
And a ladybug that was red and brown

Was up on a little stem waiting there,
And I got some rain in my hair.

—Elizabeth Madox Roberts

Who has seen the wind?
   Neither I nor you;
But when the leaves hang trembling
   The wind is passing thro'.

Who has seen the wind?
   Neither you nor I:
But when the trees bow down their heads
   The wind is passing by.

—Christina G. Rossetti

THE WIND

I saw you toss the kites on high
And blow the birds about the sky;
And all around I heard you pass,
Like ladies' skirts across the grass—
  O wind, a-blowing all day long,
  O wind, that sings so loud a song!

I saw the different things you did,
But always you yourself you hid.
I felt you push, I heard you call,
I could not see yourself at all—
  O wind, a-blowing all day long,
  O wind, that sings so loud a song!

O you that are so strong and cold,
O blower, are you young or old?
Are you a beast of field and tree,
Or just a stronger child than me?
  O wind, a-blowing all day long,
  O wind, that sings so loud a song!
            —*Robert Louis Stevenson*

FOG

The fog comes
on little cat feet.

It sits looking
over harbor and city
on silent haunches
and then moves on.
            —*Carl Sandburg*

ALMOST

There are things you almost see
    In the woods of evening—
Fairies as thick as fireflies,
    Elves leaping in a ring.

There are things you almost hear
    When no one passes by—
Stirring of seeds in good damp earth,
    Stars marching through the sky.
                              —*Rachel Field*

SUNSET AND SUNRISE

I'll tell you how the sun rose,—
A ribbon at a time.
The steeples swam in amethyst,
The news like squirrels ran.

The hills untied their bonnets,
The bobolinks begun.
Then I said softly to myself,
"That must have been the sun!"

But how it set, I know not.
There seemed a purple stile
Which little yellow boys and girls
Were climbing all the while.

Till when they reached the other side,
A dominie in gray
Put gently up the evening bars,
And led the flock away.
                              —*Emily Dickinson*

APRIL RAIN

It is not raining rain to me,
It's raining daffodils;
In every dimpled drop I see
Wild flowers on the hills.

The clouds of gray engulf the day
And overwhelm the town;
It is not raining rain to me,
It's raining roses down.

It is not raining rain to me,
But fields of clover bloom,
Where any buccaneering bee
Can find a bed and room.

A health unto the happy,
A fig for him who frets!
It is not raining rain to me,
It's raining violets.

—Robert Loveman

THE SEA BIRD TO THE WAVE

On and on,
O white brother!
Thunder does not daunt thee!
How thou movest!
By thine impulse—
With no wing!
Fairest thing
The wide sea shows me!
On and on,
O white brother!

Art thou gone?

—Padraic Colum

RUNE OF RICHES

I have a golden ball,
A big, bright, shining one,
Pure gold; and it is all
Mine.—It is the sun.

I have a silver ball,
A white and glistening stone
That other people call
The moon;—my very own!

The jewel things that prick
My cushion's soft blue cover
Are mine,—my stars, thick, thick,
Scattered the sky all over.

And everything that's mine
Is yours, and yours, and yours,—
The shimmer and the shine!—
Let's lock our wealth out-doors!
                    —*Florence Converse*

SALUT AU MONDE!

I see a great round wonder rolling through space,

. . . .

I see the shaded part on one side where the sleepers are sleep-
    ing, and the sunlit part on the other side,
I see the curious, rapid change of the light and shade,
And distant lands, as real and near to the inhabitants of them
    as my land is to me.
                    —*Walt Whitman*

I WANDERED LONELY AS A CLOUD

I wandered lonely as a cloud
That floats on high o'er vales and hills,
When all at once I saw a crowd,
A host, of golden daffodils;
Beside the lake, beneath the trees,
Fluttering and dancing in the breeze.

Continuous as the stars that shine
And twinkle on the milky way,
They stretched in never-ending line
Along the margin of a bay:
Ten thousand saw I at a glance,
Tossing their heads in sprightly dance.

The waves beside them danced; but they
Outdid the sparkling waves in glee;
A poet could not but be gay,
In such a jocund company;
I gazed—and gazed—but little thought
What wealth the show to me had brought:

For oft, when on my couch I lie
In vacant or in pensive mood,
They flash upon that inward eye
Which is the bliss of solitude;
And then my heart with pleasure fills
And dances with the daffodils.

—*William Wordsworth*

A PSALM OF DAVID
Psalm XXIII

The Lord is my shepherd; I shall not want.

He maketh me to lie down in green pastures: he leadeth me beside the still waters.

He restoreth my soul; he leadeth me in the paths of righteousness for his name's sake.

Yea, though I walk through the valley of the shadow of death, I will fear no evil: for thou *art* with me; thy rod and thy staff they comfort me.

Thou preparest a table before me in the presence of mine enemies: thou anointest my head with oil; my cup runneth over.

Surely goodness and mercy shall follow me all the days of my life: and I will dwell in the house of the Lord for ever.

A PSALM OF PRAISE
Psalm C

Make a joyful noise unto the Lord, all ye lands.

Serve the Lord with gladness: come before his presence with singing.

Know ye that the Lord he *is* God: *it is* he that hath made us, and not we ourselves: *we are* his people, and the sheep of his pasture.

Enter into his gates with thanksgiving, *and* into his courts with praises: be thankful unto him *and* bless his name.

For the Lord *is* good; his mercy *is* everlasting; and his truth *endureth* to all generations.

"SING A SONG OF SEASONS!
    SOMETHING BRIGHT IN ALL!"

AUTUMN FIRES

In the other gardens
   And all up the vale,
From the autumn bonfires
   See the smoke trail!

Pleasant summer over
   And all the summer flowers,
The red fire blazes,
   The grey smoke towers.

Sing a song of seasons!
   Something bright in all!
Flowers in the summer,
   Fires in the fall!
       —*Robert Louis Stevenson*

DOWN! DOWN!

Down, down!
Yellow and brown
The leaves are falling over the town.
       —*Eleanor Farjeon*

Fly away, fly away over the sea,
   Sun-loving swallow, for summer is done;
Come again, come again, come back to me,
Bringing the summer and bringing the sun.
       —*Christina G. Rossetti*

AUTUMN WOODS

I like the woods
   In autumn
When dry leaves hide the ground,
When the trees are bare
And the wind sweeps by
With a lonesome rushing sound.

I can rustle the leaves
   In autumn
And I can make a bed
In the thick dry leaves
That have fallen
From the bare trees
Overhead.

             —*James S. Tippett*

SEPTEMBER

A road like brown ribbon,
A sky that is blue,
A forest of green
With that sky peeping through.

Asters, deep purple,
A grasshopper's call,
Today it is summer,
Tomorrow is fall.

             —*Edwina Fallis*

SPLINTER

The voice of the last cricket
across the first frost
is one kind of good-by.
It is so thin a splinter of singing.

Carl Sandburg

COVER

Red leaves flutter,
Yellow leaves fall,
Brown leaves gather
Along a wall.

Brown leaves huddle
Against the grey
Stones some farmer
Set one way

Between two pastures.
Curled leaves keep
Any wall warm
When winter's deep.

—Frances M. Frost

ICE

When it is the winter time
I run up the street
And I make the ice laugh
With my little feet—
"Crickle, crackle, crickle
Crrreeet, crrreeet, crrreeet."

—Dorothy Aldis

WILLOWS IN THE SNOW

The willows hanging low,
Shake from their long and trailing
skirts
The freshly fallen snow.

—*Tsūrū*

WHITE FIELDS

(1)

In the winter time we go
Walking in the fields of snow;

Where there is no grass at all;
Where the top of every wall,

Every fence, and every tree,
Is as white as white can be.

(2)

Pointing out the way we came,
—Every one of them the same—

All across the fields there be
Prints in silver filigree;

And our mothers always know,
By the footprints in the snow,

Where it is the children go.

—*James Stephens*

SNOW TOWARD EVENING

Suddenly the sky turned gray,
The day,
Which had been bitter and chill,
Grew soft and still.
Quietly
From some invisible blossoming tree
Millions of petals cool and white
Drifted and blew,
Lifted and flew,
Fell with the falling night.

—*Melville Cane*

WINTER RUNE

Unriddle me my riddle
If you would have my love:
What is warm to all beneath
And cold to all above?

What moves gentle as a girl,
And has waves like the sea,
And is lighter than a butterfly,
But yet will break a tree?

What closes many a door,
As strongly as a bar,
And silences the footfalls,
And shines like a star?

And makes blossoms bloom
Where no blossoms were,
And pleases dogs and children
And the philosopher?

—*Elizabeth Coatsworth*

For, lo, the winter is past, the rain is over and gone;
The flowers appear on the earth;
The time of the singing of birds is come.
                                    —*Song of Solomon* II.

WRITTEN IN MARCH

The Cock is crowing,
The stream is flowing,
The small birds twitter,
The lake doth glitter,
The green field sleeps in the sun;
The oldest and youngest
Are at work with the strongest;
The cattle are grazing,
Their heads never raising;
There are forty feeding like one!

Like an army defeated
The snow hath retreated,
And now doth fare ill
On the top of the bare hill;
The ploughboy is whooping—anon—anon:
There's joy in the mountains;
There's life in the fountains;
Small clouds are sailing,
Blue sky prevailing;
The rain is over and gone!
                                    —*William Wordsworth*

PRAIRIE SPRING

A gray grassy hill,
A wind fresh and strong,
Blue bells, sand lilies,
A meadow lark's song.

Young sage crushed by
Tiny feet gathering flowers,
Only a prairie child
Knows such sweet hours.
            —*Edwina Fallis*

SPRING

Sound the flute!
Now 'tis mute!
Birds delight,
Day and night,
Nightingale,
In the dale,
Lark in sky—
Merrily,
Merrily, merrily to welcome in the year.

Little boy,
Full of joy;
Little girl
Sweet and small;
Cock does crow,
So do you;
Merry voice,
Infant noise;
Merrily, merrily to welcome in the year.
            —*William Blake*

THE DAY BEFORE APRIL

The day before April
    Alone, alone,
I walked in the woods
    And sat on a stone.

I sat on a broad stone
    And sang to the birds.
The tune was God's making
    But I made the words.
        —Mary Carolyn Davies

WISE JOHNNY

Little Johnny-jump-up said,
"It must be spring,
I just saw a lady-bug
And heard a robin sing."
        —Edwina Fallis

SONG FROM "APRIL"

I know
    Where the wind flowers blow!
I know,
    I have been
Where the wild honey bees
    Gather honey for their queen!

I would be
    A wild flower,
Blue sky over me,
    For an hour . . . an hour!
So the wild bees
    Should seek and discover me,
And kiss me . . . kiss me . . . kiss me!
    Not one of the dusky dears should miss me!

I know
   Where the wind flowers blow!
I know,
   I have been
Where the little rabbits run
   In the warm, yellow sun!

Oh, to be a wild flower
For an hour . . . an hour . . .
   In the heather!
A bright flower, a wild flower,
   Blown by the weather!

I know,
   I have been
Where the wild honey bees
   Gather honey for their queen!
                    —*Irene Rutherford McLeod*

APRIL AND MAY

April is a laundress
Mixing silver suds
To rinse the lacy dance frocks
Of apple-blossom buds.

May Day is the nursemaid
Who looks the flowers over
And ties their little bonnets
On the buttercup and clover.
                    —*Anne Robinson*

SPRING

When from her winter-prison
Spring comes forth,
In the morning
The white dew falls;
In the evening
The mists trail,
And in the valley of Hatsu-se
Beneath the twigs of the trees,
The nightingale sings.
                    —*Japanese Hokku*

HAREBELLS IN JUNE

Ring slender bells an elfin tune,
To summon all the elves of June;
It's time to make the plans for summertime,
Chime, little bells, along the river, chime;
And let me lie with ear close to the ground,
To hear the witching sound.

Ring slender bells this bonny weather,
Call all the elves of June together.

—Annette Wynne

THE CITY OF FALLING LEAVES

Leaves fall,
  Brown leaves,
Yellow leaves streaked with brown.
They fall,
  Flutter,
  Fall again.
  The brown leaves
    And the streaked yellow leaves
      Loosen on their branches
      And drift slowly downward.
      One,
      One, two, three,
      One, two, five.
      All Venice is a falling of autumn leaves,
      Brown, and yellow streaked with brown.

—Amy Lowell

THRENODY

The red leaves fell upon the lake,
The brown leaves drift,
The yellow leaves fly with the wind,
High and swift.

And autumn nights bring open fires,
With roasted corn,
When silver frosted grasses greet
Early morn.

I fly my kite across the hill,
The slim string breaks,
It flashes like a cloud above
Hills and lakes.

I cannot follow, only stand
And watch it go,
Across the far and lonely place
That airplanes know.

                                    —*John Farrar*

"COME CHRISTMAS THE MORN!"

CRADLE HYMN

Away in a manger,
No crib for a bed,
The little Lord Jesus
Lay down his sweet head;
The stars in the heavens
Looked down where he lay,
The little Lord Jesus
Asleep in the hay.

The cattle are lowing,
The poor baby wakes,
But little Lord Jesus
No crying he makes.
I love thee, Lord Jesus,
Look down from the sky,
And stay by my cradle
Till morning is nigh.
                                    —*Martin Luther*

A CHRISTMAS FOLK-SONG

The little Jesus came to town;
The wind blew up, the wind blew down;
Out in the street the wind was bold;
Now who would house Him from the cold?

Then opened wide the stable door,
Fair were the rushes on the floor;
The Ox put forth a hornèd head:
"Come, little Lord, here make Thy bed."

Up rose the Sheep were folded near:
"Thou Lamb of God, come, enter here."
He entered there to rush and reed,
Who was the Lamb of God indeed.

The little Jesus came to town;
With ox and sheep He laid Him down;
Peace to the byre, peace to the fold,
For that they housed Him from the cold!
                    —*Lizette Woodworth Reese*

In the bleak mid-winter
    Frosty wind made moan,
Earth stood hard as iron,
    Water like a stone;
Snow had fallen, snow on snow,
    Snow on snow,
In the bleak **mid-winter**
    Long ago.
                    —*Christina G. Rossetti*

CHRISTMAS MORNING

If Bethlehem were here today,
Or this were very long ago,
There wouldn't be a winter time
Nor any cold or snow.

I'd run out through the garden gate,
And down along the pasture walk;
And off beside the cattle barns
I'd hear a kind of gentle talk.

I'd move the heavy iron chain
And pull away the wooden pin;
I'd push the door a little bit
And tiptoe very softly in.

The pigeons and the yellow hens
And all the cows would stand away;
Their eyes would open wide to see
A lady in the manger hay.

If this were very long ago
And Bethlehem were here today.

And Mother held my hand and smiled—
I mean the lady would—and she
Would take the woolly blankets off
Her little boy so I could see.

His shut-up eyes would be asleep,
And he would look like our John,
And he would be all crumpled too,
And have a pinkish color on.

I'd watch his breath go in and out.
His little clothes would all be white.
I'd slip my finger in his hand
To feel how he could hold it tight.

And she would smile and say, "Take care,"
The mother, Mary, would, "Take care";
And I would kiss his little hand
And touch his hair.

While Mary put the blankets back
The gentle talk would soon begin.
And when I'd tiptoe softly out
I'd meet the wise men going in.

—*Elizabeth Madox Roberts*

THE WAITS

There were sparkles on the windowpane and sparkles in the
    sky,
The moon it sparkled like a star above the world so high,
There was starshine on the ceiling, there was starshine on
    the bed,
There was starshine in my eyes, I think, and starshine in my
    head.

I clambered from my sleep, I did; and flung the window
    wide,
I wanted all that waited in the Christmas Eve outside,
I wanted for myself to hear the Christmas people sing,
I wanted for myself to hear the Christmas joy bells ring.

And there outside were waiting three grey Shepherds in the
snow
(I knew that they were Shepherds, for they all had crooks,
you know),
And when they saw me waiting too, they sang to me a song—
The stars they caught and whispered it the whole wide sky
along.

And then the Shepherds went their way and three black
camels came,
They stayed beneath the window there and waited just the
same,
And each black camel on his back had brought an Eastern
King,
And though each King was very rich each had a song to sing.

They sang it as the Shepherds sang, a little low, sweet song—
The white stars caught and whispered it the whole wide sky
along;
And then the camels went their way, I watched them down
the street,
The snow lay white and soft and still beneath their silent
feet.

There was singing in the treetops, there was singing in the
sky,
The moon was singing to the clouds above the world so high,
And all the stars were singing too, and when I looked below,
I saw a little tiny Child was waiting in the snow.

At first I watched Him wait there—watched and only waved
my hand,
For though the song was in my heart I did not understand,
Until at last it burst in words, because at last I knew,
And then he laughed and looked at me and sang the star
song too.

And right across the misty fields I heard the church bells
    ring,
The star song echoed far and wide for all the world to sing,
But still the tiny Child stood there—the Child that once was
    born—
We sang His birthday song, we did, upon His birthday
    morn.

—*M. Nightingale*

A CHRISTMAS PRAYER

Loving looks the large-eyed cow,
Loving stares the long-eared ass,
At Heaven's glory in the grass!
Child, with added human birth
Come to bring the child of earth
Glad repentance, tearful mirth,
And a seat beside the hearth
At the Father's knee—
Make us peaceful as thy cow;
Make us patient as thine ass;
Make us quiet as thou art now;
Make us strong as thou wilt be.
Make us always know and see
We are his, as well as thou.

—*George MacDonald*

EX ORE INFANTIUM

Little Jesus, wast Thou shy
Once, and just so small as I?
And what did it feel like to be
Out of Heaven, and just like me?
Didst Thou sometimes think of *there*,
And ask where all the angels were?
I should think that I would cry
For my house all made of sky;
I would look about the air,
And wonder where my angels were;
And at waking 'twould distress me—
Not an angel there to dress me!

Hadst Thou ever any toys,
Like us little girls and boys?
And didst Thou play in Heaven with all
The angels, that were not too tall,
With stars for marbles? Did the things
Play *Can you see me?* through their wings?

Didst Thou kneel at night to pray,
And didst Thou join Thy hands, this way?
And did they tire sometimes, being young,
And make the prayer seem very long?
And dost Thou like it best, that we
Should join our hands to pray to Thee?
I used to think, before I knew,
The prayer not said unless we do.
And did Thy Mother at the night
Kiss Thee, and fold the clothes in right?
And didst Thou feel quite good in bed,
Kissed and sweet, and Thy prayers said?

Thou canst not have forgotten all
That it feels like to be small;
And Thou know'st I cannot pray
To Thee in my father's way—
When Thou wast so little, say,
Couldst Thou talk Thy Father's way?
So, a little Child, come down
And hear a child's tongue like Thy own;
Take me by the hand and walk,
And listen to my baby-talk.
To Thy Father show my prayer
(He will look, Thou art so fair),
And say: "O Father, I, Thy Son,
Bring the prayer of a little one."

And He will smile, that children's tongue
Hast not changed since Thou wast young!
—Francis Thompson

EARTH AND SKY
(They talk to each other on Christmas Eve.)

Earth. Oh Sky, you look so drear!
Sky. Oh Earth, you look so bare!
Earth. How chilly you appear!
Sky. How empty you lie there!

Sky. My winds blow icy cold.
Earth. My flowers have gone from me.
Sky. Yet I've one Star of gold.
Earth. And I have one green Tree.

Sky. I'll set my Star on high
Alone in its own light
For any Child to spy
Who wakes on Christmas Night.

Earth. I'll hang my Tree with toys,
Like fruit and flowers gay,
For little girls and boys
To pick on Christmas Day.

They Then let the soft snow fall,
say to- And let the cold wind blow!
gether We have in spite of all
A pretty thing to show.

Yes, Christmas Eve and Morn
We'll show our pretty thing
To every baby born
Of Beggar-man or King.

Earth. Oh Sky, you look so clear!
Sky. Oh Earth, you look so fair!
Earth. How bright your Star shines here.
Sky. How green your tree grows there.

—*Eleanor Farjeon*

NOW EVERY CHILD

Now every Child that dwells on earth,
  Stand up, stand up and sing!
The passing night has given birth
  Unto the Children's King.
     Sing sweet as the flute,
     Sing clear as the horn,
     Sing joy of the Children
     Come Christmas the morn!
     Little Christ Jesus
     Our Brother is born.

Now every Star that dwells in sky,
  Look down with shining eyes!
The night has dropped in passing by
  A Star from Paradise.
     Sing sweet as the flute,
     Sing clear as the horn,
     Sing joy of the Stars
     Come Christmas the morn!
     Little Christ Jesus
     Our Brother is born.

Now every Beast that crops in field,
  Breathe sweetly and adore!
The night has brought the richest yield
  That ever harvest bore.
     Sing sweet as the flute,
     Sing clear as the horn,
     Sing joy of the Creatures
     Come Christmas the morn!
     Little Christ Jesus
     Our Brother is born.

Now every Bird that flies in air,
  Sing, raven, lark and dove!
The night has brooded on her lair
  And fledged the Bird of Love.
    Sing sweet as the flute,
    Sing clear as the horn,
    Sing joy of the Birds
    Come Christmas the morn!
    Little Christ Jesus
    Our Brother is born.

Now all the Angels of the Lord
  Rise up on Christmas Even!
The passing night will bear the Word
  That is the Voice of Heaven.
    Sing sweet as the flute,
    Sing clear as the horn,
    Sing joy of the Angels
    Come Christmas the morn!
    Little Christ Jesus
    Our Brother is born.

                    —*Eleanor Farjeon*

A CHRISTMAS CAROL

The Christ-child lay on Mary's lap,
   His hair was like a light.
(O weary, weary were the world,
   But here is all aright.)

The Christ-child lay on Mary's breast,
   His hair was like a star.
(O stern and cunning are the kings,
   But here the true hearts are.)

The Christ-child lay on Mary's heart,
   His hair was like a fire.
(O weary, weary is the world,
   But here the world's desire.)

The Christ-child stood at Mary's knee,
   His hair was like a crown,
And all the flowers looked up at Him
   And all the stars looked down.

                —*Gilbert K. Chesterton*

"GOOD NIGHT! GOOD NIGHT!
FAR FLIES THE LIGHT."

GOOD NIGHT

Good night! good night!
Far flies the light;
But still God's love
Shall flame above,
Making all bright.
Good night! Good night!
—*Victor Hugo*

THE BALLAD OF DOWNAL BAUN
(Domhnal Ban)

The moon-cradle's rocking and rocking,
Where a cloud and a cloud goes by:
Silently rocking and rocking,
The moon-cradle out in the sky.
—*Padraic Colum*

THE SLEEPY SONG

As soon as the fire burns red and low,
And the house upstairs is still,
She sings me a queer little sleepy song,
Of sheep that go over the hill.

The good little sheep run quick and soft,
Their colors are gray and white:
They follow their leader nose to tail,
For they must be home by night.

And one slips over and one comes next,
And one runs after behind,
The gray one's nose at the white one's tail,
The top of the hill they find.

And when they get to the top of the hill
They quietly slip away,
But one runs over and one comes next—
Their colors are white and gray.

And over they go, and over they go,
And over the top of the hill,
The good little sheep run quick and soft,
And the house upstairs is still.

And one slips over and one comes next,
The good little, gray little sheep!
I watch how the fire burns red and low,
And she says that I fall asleep.
                    —*Josephine Daskam Bacon*

THE WHITE WINDOW

The Moon comes every night to peep
Through the window where I lie:
But I pretend to be asleep;
And watch the Moon go slowly by,
—And she never makes a sound!

She stands and stares! And then she goes
To the house that's next to me,
Stealing by on tippy-toes;
To peep at folk asleep maybe
—And she never makes a sound!
                    —*James Stephens*

CRADLE HYMN

Hush! my dear, lie still and slumber;
   Holy angels guard thy bed;
Heavenly blessings without number,
   Gently falling on thy head.

How much better thou'rt attended
   Than the Son of God could be,
When from heaven he descended
   And became a child like thee!

Soft and easy is thy cradle:
   Coarse and hard thy Saviour lay,
When his birthplace was u stable,
   And his softest bed was hay.

See the kindly shepherds round him,
   Telling wonders from the sky!
Where they sought him, there they found him,
   With his Virgin Mother by.

See the lovely babe a-dressing,
   Lovely infant, how he smiled,
When He wept, the mother's blessing
   Soothed and hushed the holy Child.

Lo, he slumbers in the manger,
   Where the hornèd oxen fed,
Peace, my darling, here's no danger,
   Here's no oxen near thy bed.

—Isaac Watts

NORSE LULLABY

The sky is dark and the hills are white
As the storm-king speeds from the north to-night;
And this is the song the storm-king sings,
As over the world his cloak he flings:
  "Sleep, sleep, little one, sleep";
He rustles his wings and gruffly sings:
  "Sleep, little one, sleep."

On yonder mountain-side a vine
Clings at the foot of a mother pine;
The tree bends over the trembling thing,
And only the vine can hear her sing:
  "Sleep, sleep, little one, sleep—
What shall you fear when I am here?
  Sleep, little one, sleep."

The king may sing in his bitter flight,
The tree may croon to the vine to-night,
But the little snowflake at my breast
Liketh the song I sing the best—
  Sleep, sleep, little one, sleep;
Weary thou art, a-next my heart
  Sleep, little one, sleep.

—*Eugene Field*

CHECK

The Night was creeping on the ground!
She crept and did not make a sound,

Until she reached the tree: And then
She covered it, and stole again

Along the grass beside the wall!
—I heard the rustling of her shawl

As she threw blackness everywhere
Along the sky, the ground, the air,

And in the room where I was hid!
But, no matter what she did

To everything that was without,
She could not put my candle out!

So I stared at the Night! And she
Stared back solemnly at me!
—*James Stephens*

THE MOON'S THE NORTH WIND'S COOKY

The Moon's the North Wind's cooky,
He bites it, day by day,
Until there's but a rim of scraps
That crumble all away.

The South Wind is a baker.
He kneads clouds in his den,
And bakes a crisp new moon *that . . . greedy*
North . . . Wind . . . eats . . . again!
—*Vachel Lindsay*

[189]

CRESCENT MOON

And Dick said, "Look what I have found!"
And when we saw we danced around,
And made our feet just tip the ground.

We skipped our toes and sang, "Oh-lo.
Oh-who, oh-who, oh what do you know!
Oh-who, oh-hi, oh-loo, kee-lo!"

We clapped our hands and sang, "Oh-ee!"
It made us jump and laugh to see
The little new moon above the tree.
                    —*Elizabeth Madox Roberts*

THE FALLING STAR

I saw a star slide down the sky,
Blinding the north as it went by,
Too lovely to be bought or sold,
Too burning and too quick to hold,
Good only to make wishes on
And then forever to be gone.
                    —*Sara Teasdale*

SILVER

Slowly, silently, now the moon
Walks the night in her silver shoon;
This way, and that, she peers, and sees
Silver fruit upon silver trees;
One by one the casements catch
Her beams beneath the silvery thatch;
Couched in his kennel, like a log,
With paws of silver sleeps the dog;
From their shadowy cote the white breasts peep
Of doves in a silver-feathered sleep;
A harvest mouse goes scampering by,
With silver claws, and silver eye;
And moveless fish in the water gleam,
By silver reeds in a silver stream.

—Walter de la Mare

NIGHT

Stars over snow,
    And in the west a planet
Swinging below a star—
    Look for a lovely thing and you will find it,
It is not far—
    It never will be far.

—Sara Teasdale

SUNG
UNDER THE
SILVER UMBRELLA

Compiled by the Literature Committee

of the

ASSOCIATION FOR CHILDHOOD EDUCATION *

1932–1935

JEAN BETZNER, *Teachers College, Columbia University*

FRANCES KERN, *National College of Education*

ELOISE RAMSEY, *Wayne University*

MARTHA SEELING, *Pestalozzi-Froebel Teachers College*

ETHEL B. WARING, *New York State College of Home Economics, Cornell University*

ADAH WHITCOMB, *Chicago Public Library*

MARY REED WOOD, *Trenton Public Schools*

MARY LINCOLN MORSE, Chairman

* The Association for Childhood Education became The Association for Childhood Education International in 1946.

A MESSAGE TO GROWN-UPS BY WAY OF EXPLANATION

THE Literature Committee of the Association for Childhood Education has for the past three years been compiling an anthology of verse for children of the nursery school, kindergarten and primary ages.

Earlier in its experience as a committee came the publishing of *Told under the Green Umbrella,* a carefully selected group of stories chosen out of the Selected List of stories and story sources published for the Association by a previous committee. In *Told under the Green Umbrella* were gathered tales that were folk or fairy in type, tales such as your mother told you and her mother told her; and so on back into the days when someone, childlike in spirit, in interest and in story-sense, conceived the story that has lasted from generation to generation and that should be a part of the literary heritage of every child.

By the time *Told under the Green Umbrella* had reached its printing state, the Literature Committee was already selecting, instead of the folk or fairy story brought nightly by Olé Luköie under his umbrella to all good children, every day stories—stories so close to each child's actual experience that although they might deal with other boys and girls and what happened to them, they might as naturally have happened to him; stories of the "here and now," of the actual (or nearly so), of the "it might have happened to me" type believed so basic in the life of the child of today. Complemented by, and in many cases patterned upon the story form preserved from generation to generation in the folk or fairy tale, the "here and now" story brings to the modern child the life that is today. Together our Green and Blue Umbrella books cover the story field for children.

While our second, or Blue Umbrella, was at the press, the members of the Literature Committee had left the story field with its two-sided imaginative approach to reach into the lovely realm of verse, and if verse is to be both wisely and happily presented for the most appreciative child age, *Sung under the Silver Umbrella* has resulted.

There has been much less committee unanimity in the choosing of verse than in the selecting of stories, partly because verse covers so wide a range but even more largely in that, because of its own spirit and freedom, poetry defies a common definition. What is poetry to one human being does not touch the same responsive chord in another. It is even true, of each one of us, that in varying moods we respond quite differently to one and the same bit of verse. If this is true of us it is equally true of children.

Without so nominating poetry's difficulty of definition in the bond, we have at no place along the way tried to seek a common definition; such definition as lies under the choice of the verse included in *Sung under the Silver Umbrella* is imbedded in the verse itself. Every poem, unless known by heart, has been copied and sent to each committee member. One negative committee vote in connection with its verse has brought with it a reconsideration. Every poem included today in *Sung under the Silver Umbrella* has a majority committee sanction and has easily won its place under our Umbrella.

For some time in our committee correspondence we debated the wisdom of the inclusion of some of the Mother Goose rhymes and jingles in our anthology; we recognize Mother Goose as the matchless earliest verse heritage of children; its rhymes are so well known to you that it was decided to omit Mother Goose. Under "Higgledy Piggledy O" we have placed verse akin to it in sound, in movement and the joy of its nonsense.

[195]

Some of our verse is cadenced and unrhymed, a verse form natural to all children and their own freest verse expression. Other verse has a distinct and dearly loved rhythmic and rhymed pattern. Some may seem a bit prosaic in interest and in attitude, while still more is delicately lovely in its picture, its interpretation, its mood and its music. In many cases, in choosing verse, we have crossed the usual eight-year-old-age line. Who knows where this is, in poetic response, for the individual child? And shouldn't poetry, of all things, reach forward and become a part of one's innermost self, lying fallow as it awaits fuller appreciation at a riper age?

Some bits of verse sought by our committee proved unattainable; a striking example of this is the verse of Milne. You will miss, as we do, many we had hoped to include. Again, as a committee, we want you to know that even the copyright allowance of a rarely generous publisher did not cover our chosen verse. With thoughtfully weighed poem at stake, confined by copyright charges, the cutting down and cutting out of any became a matter of very serious concern. Choosing verse is a delicate art and doubly so when verse must be chosen from verse already weighed and found wanted.

In closing this committee explanation as to how *Sung under the Silver Umbrella* came to be, and in its present form, we are glad both for ourselves and you that it was possible to include as a foreword so discerning an interpretative essay by Padraic Colum, and again that Dorothy Lathrop could be secured to decorate our Silver Umbrella in so charmingly poetic a manner.

—MARY LINCOLN MORSE

1935

ACKNOWLEDGMENTS

For permission to reprint the poems included in *Sung under the Silver Umbrella* the Literature Committee of The Association for Childhood Education records its appreciation to the following:—

D. Appleton-Century Company, Inc., New York, for "The Waits," from *Fifty Christmas Poems for Children* by M. Nightingale.

The Book House for Children, Chicago, for "A Shower," "Colts," "Lilies," "The Rains of Spring," "Daffodils," "Plum Blossoms" and "Spring," from *Little Pictures of Japan.*

Brandt & Brandt, New York, for "Wonder Where the Horseshoe Went," from *Poems Selected for Young People.* Published by Harper & Brothers (Copyright, 1929, by Edna St. Vincent Millay); "The Unexplorer," from *A Few Figs from Thistles.* Published by Harper & Brothers (Copyright, 1923, by Edna St. Vincent Millay).

Coward McCann, Inc., New York, for "Counters" and "The Mouse," from *Compass Rose* by Elizabeth Coatsworth.

The John Day Company, Inc., New York, for "Stop—Go," from *I Like Automobiles* by Dorothy W. Baruch.

Dodd, Mead & Company, Inc., New York, for "A Christmas Carol," from *The Collected Poems of G. K. Chesterton;* "Ex Ore Infantium" by Francis Thompson; "Mr. Moon," from *A Song of the Little People* by Bliss Carman; "Called Away" by Richard Le Gallienne.

[197]

Moon's the North Wind's Cooky," from *Collected Poems* by Vachel Lindsay; "An Evening Falls," "Breakfast Time," "Check," "The White Window" and "White Fields," from *Collected Poems* by James Stephens; "The Rabbits' Song outside the Tavern," from *Away Goes Sally* by Elizabeth Coatsworth; "Cat" and "Shore," from *Menagerie* by Mary Britton Miller; "Brown and Furry," "A City Mouse," "Ferry Me across the Water," "Fly Away," "The Horses of the Sea," "In the Bleak Mid-winter," "Minnie and Mattie," "Mix a Pancake," "What Does the Bee Do?," "What Is Pink?," "Who Has Seen the Wind?" and "Wrens and Robins in the Hedge," from *Sing-Song* by Christina G. Rossetti; "Night" and "The Falling Star," from *Stars To-night* by Sara Teasdale; "A Summer Morning," "The Little Rose Tree" and "Almost," from *The Pointed People* by Rachel Field; "The Swing," "At the Sea-Side," "Singing," "My Ship and I," "Where Go the Boats?," "The Cow," "Foreign Lands," "Rain," "The Wind" and "Autumn Fires," from *A Child's Garden of Verses* by Robert Louis Stevenson.

Minton, Balch & Co., New York, for "Feet," "Hands," "Hiding," "Ice" and "Little," from *Everything and Anything* and "Names," from *Hop, Skip and Jump* by Dorothy Aldis.

James Nisbet & Co., Ltd., London, for "The Merry Man of Paris" by Stella Mead.

Oxford University Press, London, for "Herons" and "Willows in the Snow," from *A Year of Japanese Epigrams* by William N. Porter.

A. D. Peters, London, for "The Blackbird" by Humbert Wolfe.

The Poetry Review, the journal of The Poetry Society, Inc., London, for "Scarecrow" by Michael Franklin.

The Saturday Review of Literature, New York, for "Winter Rune" by Elizabeth Coatsworth.

Charles Scribner's Sons, New York, for "The Sleepy Song," from *Poems* by Josephine Daskam Bacon; "Norse Lullaby," from *With Trumpet and Drums* by Eugene

[201]

Marie Louise Allen, for "Mitten Song" and "My Zipper Suit."

Beatrice Bergquist, for "The Song of the Robin."

Florence Converse, for "Rune of Riches," from *A Masque of Sibyls,* published by Houghton Mifflin Company.

Bridgham Curtis, for "Wind-Song," "Hopi Lullaby," "Corn-Grinding Song—Laguna Indians," and "Corn-Grinding Song—Zuñi Indians," from *The Indians' Book* by Natalie Curtis (Copyright, 1907, by Natalie Curtis; copyright, 1923, by Paul Burlin), published by Harper & Brothers.

Edwina Fallis, for "Wise Johnny," "Prairie Spring" and "September."

John Flexman, for "The Shiny Little House" by Nancy M. Hayes.

Winifred Howard, for "White Horses" and "Fairy Wings," from *Out of the Everywhere,* published by Oxford University Press.

Alice L. Hubbard, for "New Shoes," from *The Golden Flute* by Alice Wilkins.

Louis Loveman for "April Rain" by Robert Loveman.

Thomas Bird Mosher, Maine, for "A Christmas Folk-Song," from *A Wayside Lute* by Lizette Woodworth Reese.

Norreys Jephson O'Conor, for "In the Moonlight," from *Songs of the Celtic Past.*

Seumas O'Sullivan, for "The Milkman."

Lucy Fitch Perkins, for "Honey Bee."

Dorothy Mason Pierce, for "Sprinkling."

Laura E. Richards and *Child Life,* Chicago, for "The High Barbaree."

Anne Robinson and Oglethorpe University, for "April and May," "To Laddie," "The Drummer" and "Conversation," from *Little Miss April.*

Lillian Schulz, for "Fuzzy Wuzzy, Creepy Crawly."

Muriel Sipe, for "Good-morning."

Miriam Weatherley, for "The Tale of a Tart" by Frederick E. Weatherley.

INDEX OF AUTHORS

[205]

INDEX OF FIRST LINES